My Affair with Mickey

By Tami Casias

An unofficial novel based on a true dream

OOMM Books
Sonoma, CA, 95476, USA
First Printing, April 2014
5 4 3 2 1

Cover design by Teresa Casias and Sean Madden
Cover photograph by Benjamin Casias

Publisher's note:

This is a work of fiction. Except for the character
names and public areas of Disneyland, names,
characters, places, incidents and behind-the-scenes park
areas either are the product of the author's imagination
or are used fictitiously, any resemblance to actual
persons, living or dead, other business establishments,
events or locales are entirely coincidental.

To my husband Glenn for his continued love and support.

To Benjamin, Teresa, Caroline and Joseph—who let me pretend all those times, we were going to the park for them.

Chapter One

On a Disneyland morning when I was a kid, I'd jump into clothes set out the day before, inhale the mandatory breakfast and be the first to buckle in the car. As a mature adult, I snagged something clean off the unfolded pile, skipped the kitchen and headed straight for the driveway.

The tiny visor mirror was large enough to coat mascara around one brown eye at a time, but too small to tell if I'd managed to pin up all my mousey shoulder-length hair. I rubbed on foundation and blush by memory while my husband slid behind the wheel, his spiky blond crew cut still glistening from the long shower after his crossfit workout.

Michael lacked the amusement park gene so instead of boring him with details of the many Disneyland trips I'd taken with my parents, I listened to the voices in my head.

"We're about there, Mini," Mom said.

I heard her, Michael didn't. The mental conversations with my parents started the day the tickets arrived.

Michael's fingers tapped the steering wheel to some imaginary beat as he took the Disney Way exit from Highway 5, chatting about what the day had to offer him. I crossed and uncrossed my legs in a pattern designed to keep my racing pulse in check and to appear I was listening.

"Can you spot the Matterhorn yet?" Mom asked. "Remember the first to see it, gets to pick the first ride."

I rolled down the window and strained out to see the white pointy peak, but decades of construction blocked my view. It was too soon to see; too soon for the smell of popcorn as the Southern California fumes filled the car.

Michael and I did everything together. Except this. Today I would have a day at Disneyland alone with my memories and he would never know I'd rather not go to the park at all, than to go with someone who didn't get the magic.

The soft brush of his hand on my cheek startled me back to reality.

"Daydreaming, Babe?" Michael smiled. "Time to engage roll up. We've almost landed."

"Roger that." Michael always fell into pilot speak when excited. Combined with the increasing tenderness he'd displayed the last few weeks proved he was as keyed up about the countdown as I was.

We'd made a deal. The twenties were for us as a couple, our thirties for building a family. Three days were left until our shared birthday. I'd spend the first day at Disneyland, then two days at home planning how to convert an office into a nursery while he was at a Las Vegas convention.

I didn't marry Michael nine years ago because he understood me better than anyone else. It was his smell. The soft vanilla scent of the plastic toys at the factory where he worked. Every hug pulled me back to my warmest memories of holidays and birthdays. A promise of the fun and family we would share.

But the scent faded as he moved up from the production floor to middle management. It was replaced with the frustrated aroma of too much coffee and paperwork which brought me back to my many failed attempts to finish college.

Last month he'd splashed on a new mens' cologne. This reminded me of nothing at all, but I liked it.

Michael never let me call him Mickey and he didn't approve that my family nicknamed me Mini. He insisted on Margaret, which I'd inherited from my great aunt who had painted nudes in Arizona until she passed during a senior tango competition at ninety six. My parents weren't so lucky. They'd died in a car crash.

Mom and Dad were the best. Every birthday they would drive me the five miles to Disneyland and I'd have my picture taken with Mickey—Mom's version of a growth chart.

For Michael, Disneyland ranked next to nicknames. So even though we lived in my parents' house, minutes from the park, this was my first time back since I'd married. He didn't see any reason to pay for something I'd done so many times. I'd tried to explain. Kind of. But I couldn't put into words my love for a mouse.

It had taken dumb luck, a lie, and a secret obsession to get me here today.

Michael listened to a radio program for plane freaks and last week won box seats for an air show in Vegas by being the first to call in. Since he'd already planned to fly to Vegas that night to set up a booth for the toy convention, his company would be paying for his flight to the air show.

Then his boss announced a surprise family day at Disneyland and expected Michael to take a later flight.

"God!" Michael had cried. "Great air show tickets and I'm going to miss it for an amusement park."

"Uh, huh," I'd tried to appear sympathetic, but—just an amusement park?

"Or I could pretend to be sick or something and we could skip the whole thing."

"But, but," I'd scrambled for a quick plan powered by the fear of losing my park day. "Won't there be others at the convention who might say something?"

"That's true. I guess I'm stuck going." His bottom lip had stuck out.

"Sorry about the planes," I'd said. "But work comes first, right?"

"They're jets," he'd reminded me.

"Jets. You love them. And box seats? You can't miss this."

"Oh Margaret, you have no idea what working for a living is like." He'd made a big show of rolling up his sleeves and pulling out his model plane tool kit. "Chris is crazy enough to think I'm not a team player if I don't make it to the park."

A vision of Michael grumbling and checking his watch all day while I struggled to have a good time at Disneyland flashed into my brain and hatched a dream I'd been incubating.

"There might be another way, Michael," I'd wanted to appear more helpful than eager. "Why don't you go until the company photo then sneak out? I'd be willing to stay and pretend you're still there all day if that helped you."

"That might work." He'd spun around and took me by the shoulders. "That's asking a lot of you though. You aren't a good liar."

"I know." An inability to bend the truth was a character flaw to this three-time Salesman of the Year.

His eyes returned to his planes, giving a light spin to the suspended 1938 bomber model that had taken him two months to complete. "You finally know how to use your cell phone, so we'd be in contact all day long if you needed me."

"So it's a go?"

"Affirmative." *Yes!* I'd wormed my way into a day for myself. I'd planned to do three Hail Mary's to readjust my Karma after my altered truth. I was not Catholic, but being raised Protestant didn't leave you with any quick way to both punish then forgive yourself.

And in a few minutes, it would be me and my mouse.

Michael stopped the car at a light and a long trail of parents and children crossed Harbor Boulevard to the park side of the street. The same electricity that placed a bounce in their step was charging my heart.

"Remember I'm going to bail after they finish the company picture," Michael said. "Do we need to go over again what you're supposed to say?"

"I got it. Hang out in plain sight and if anyone asks me, tell them you're in the bathroom."

"Try to leave me a little dignity," he sighed and turned into the park. "Say I'm on a ride that you're too scared to go on."

I spotted my favorite mountain against the blue-gray sky.

"I see it Mom! I win. I get to pick the first ride."

"It's a good thing I'm getting reimbursed," Michael grumbled and forked over the cash to the parking attendant then handed me the slip and park map. I pulled the organizer Michael bought me out of my carpet-bag style purse and slid the receipt into the folder for today marked "parking" and entered the amount on the attached three-color sheet.

"Check time," Michael announced. "Purse."

"Check."

"Ticket package."

"Check." I'd been guarding them with my life since he'd brought them home.

"Stupid hats."

"Check." I tugged the bright red baseball hat over the top of my French twist that was Michael's favorite look for me.

He snatched it off and tossed it into the back seat. "That is not attractive babe."

"Check."I was not sure I had a look. My large boobs were out of proportion for my frame. Today I'd picked khaki pants and a beige top that reached my narrow hips. Michael prefers his own clothing tight, to show off regular workouts.

We walked down the parking ramp to the front entrance past waist-high green cones to the security gate where a diligent employee took five minutes to go through my large bag.

"Let's get this over—" My ears shut Michael out again when I pushed through the turn stall and came face to face with the main garden, planted in annuals in the shape of Mickey's face. I was home.

"Isn't this lovely, Mini?" Mom asked. "Let's get a picture of you with Dad."

Michael grabbed my arm and moved me to his work group where dozens of smiling Chris' Toys employees, spouses, and children waited. "This is going to be a great day," he whispered as we stood next to his boss Chris and his family—wife Emily and a teenage son who looked about as thrilled as Michael to be at the park.

"Thanks for having us, Chris." I shook his hand after the photo was complete. His round figure mimicked their bestselling children's toy, a rolling clown. "This is one of my favorite places."

"Mine too. But you're not wearing the hat," Chris said.

"She's always worried about her hair," Michael shrugged. I smoothed the wrinkled front of my colorless blouse wishing that the bright red logo shirt everyone else in the picture wore had looked good on me.

Chris' smile thinned. "You remember my wife Emily and son Luke."

Luke expressed the level of boredom only thirteen-year-olds forced on a family outing could muster. "This isn't my happiest place on Earth. There aren't even any video games."

"Oh but there are!" I was so excited to share the news. "I read that the newest X-box and Playstation games are in the Dream House at Innoventions. You should check it out."

"Cool!" Luke smiled. Michael pulled me back to his side. I talked too much, but I couldn't stop the flow of words.

"See? You're never too old for Disneyland." Chris draped an arm over Luke's shoulder, the other around a young woman. "Remember Jessica? She just finished grad school at UC Santa Barbara in marketing and is back to work with us."

"Wow, you look great!" I said. With her long blonde hair cut into a bob that angled around her face, I didn't recognize her. I had about seven years on her, but in my serviceable outfit and old hairstyle, it looked closer to seventeen.

"Thanks, Mrs. Gunderson." Jessica bent to tighten the buckle on her precarious high-heeled sandals. *She isn't going to last long on her feet today.* Jessica had always been a favorite office helper of Michael's during summer breaks and was going to be at the same convention in Vegas.

"Time for fun. Shall we all go together?" Chris grinned and pointed to an older woman next to him, who smiled as our eyes met. "This is Felicity. She's setting us up with a tour guide so we don't miss anything."

"Not me," Jessica shook her head. "I'm going to meet some friends, then catch my flight for Vegas."

"I've never been on a tour," I raised my hand, forgetting for a moment I needed to be a lone wolf.

"But we'd slow you down," Michael grabbed my arm and pulled me in the opposite direction. "Margaret doesn't do the rides. So she's going to walk through all the shops while I go on Indiana Jones first. I'll try and catch up with you later."

He pulled me down Main Street at a pace too fast to see anything but a blur of strollers.

"Hey," I slowed at a colorful prize wheel, "we should check our tickets to see if we won anything."

"There's no time."

Racing under the arched entrance to Frontierland he taxied to a stop in front of a bathroom, and peered back to see Chris, his wife and Luke walking to the opposite corner of the park in Tomorrowland behind a young guide holding a small flag. I wanted to be part of that tiny parade.

"What's your flight plan?" he asked.

"I don't know yet." I had given the park all of my attention since he'd brought home the tickets but I hadn't settled on a direction.

"You should start from right here. The Tiki Room has a show in ten minutes." He scanned the crowd again. "Okay they're out of sight."

He handed me the car keys and waited for me to zip them into the side pocket of my purse.

"The parking space number is written on the ticket in your organizer. I need you to do this one thing for me, then you can go home." He took my face in his hands. "Are you sure you can handle this?"

I didn't want to hurt his feelings with the truth that I was anxious for him to leave. It had taken the Blue Angels to blast him from my side.

"I can do it." I had the driving directions in my purse, cash for food, a lie ready for Chris, and a day with my parents at the park. Their memories anyway. "Have a great time at the air show. Maybe you'll meet one of the pilots."

His grin widened and he nodded.

9

"I'll check in with you throughout the day to make sure you're okay and that you get home. Love you." He pulled me in for a long kiss, then tucked a stray lock behind my ear. "You should duck into the bathroom first. Your hair is falling out."

Both of my hands were trying to smooth some sense of style into my hair as he hurried off.

The bathroom was already crowded, so I tightened the knot at my head and smoothed the fly away strands behind my ears without looking in the mirror before returning to the Tiki Room entrance.

The talking flowers and birds were on my list, but I wasn't ready for them. I didn't want my day to start from here. So much around me appeared familiar yet new at the same time. Michael wasn't going to chart my course today. I'd start all over again from the park gate and let Disneyland unfold for me naturally.

Today I could do anything. Like a rebel with an original Disneyland E ticket, I would have my day, my way.

I focused on the sidewalk to avoid spoiling the adventure and zigzagged upstream between strollers and a sea of park guests back to the entrance. I turned back toward Main Street when a tug pulled at my leg. I hobbled and started to fall when my shoelace caught a passing stroller. I grabbed out for support and managed to miss taking the head off the child.

"Ah!" Pain shot through my knees and hands as I hit the ground. I pushed myself up to discover a plush Mickey Mouse staring back at me in a bed of tall pink snapdragons. The sound of a crying child pulled my attention straight at a set of passing shoes. Michael's shoes—next to a pair of familiar high heels.

Detaching my shoelace from a stroller wheel, I tossed the stuffed Mickey and an apology to a crying toddler and searched for Michael. I found him. He held Jessica's hand at the exit. Michael pulled her into his arms and I stopped close enough to hear him ask "Tickets?"

"Check," she giggled.

"Kiss?"

Her lips mouthed "Check" but my hearing was gone again. Michael smiled and leaned in for a long kiss. The kind he had just given me. I was so close. If they turned they would spot me. But neither looked. When they pulled apart, he wrapped an arm over her shoulder, turned his back and walked out the exit without asking for a return hand stamp.

"I'm afraid he won't be there for you," Dad said. "He'll always put himself first."

My breaths were a ragged pant. A pounding that started in my chest radiated to my head where the thrums drowned out Dad's words.

I stayed upright only by the sheer number of people bobbing around me, supporting me.

"Excuse me, dear," an elderly woman's voice said from behind me with a light touch on my shoulder. "It's your turn."

"What?" I focused ahead on a young man dressed in a train conductor's uniform, his hand outstretched.

"It's your turn at the wheel," the woman's voice behind me repeated.

Flashing lights on the large spinning wheel drew me in.

"I'll need your ticket," the conductor said, still holding out his hand.

"Check," I squeaked.

I watched him place my ticket on the scanner. Mickey's black ears stood strong on the white paper background.

The woman's voice spoke again, with a giggle. "I have a hunch today may be your day."

The wheel spun in blurring strips of flashing lights and loud clicks. The sound typed out: "Michael has a lover. Michael has a lover." The wheel slowed, then stopped with a scream of sound—popping, whistles.

"We have a grand prize winner!" the conductor yelled.

"Huh?" I narrowed in on his young face. *What is he saying?*

"You've unlocked the Castle!"

My leg bones liquefied and tiny stars twinkled at the corner of my eyes. A blue Mickey Mouse balloon escaped higher and higher into a sky filled with confetti and then went black.

Chapter 2

"**U**mm." A cool sensation brushed my forehead waking me from the strangest dream. I stretched out against the bed when my knuckles scraped concrete. *Crap.*

"See, she's coming around," a woman's voice said. "My goodness. Who wouldn't faint after winning the Castle!"

If I don't move, people might leave and I can run out of the park, find Michael and—

A cold liquid rolled down my temple forcing my blurry eyes open.

"Are you all right? You'd probably like to freshen up," the woman asked as another sweet-smelling drip—root beer—trickled down from a green Mowgli-shaped straw she held in one hand. Her other held a twenty-four ounce sized cup printed with characters from The Jungle Book. *I must be okay or someone less silly, and probably wearing a white coat of some kind, would be taking care of me.*

"Ah-choo!" Confetti blew out my nose. I sat up to sneeze again and my vision cleared. Tiny multicolored specks of paper were still snowing down around me. I turned to look for my bag. My body had left the only bare spot on the surrounding asphalt. A corpse outline at a murder scene. I'd died and gone to Disney heaven.

A black blazer blocked out the sun and a large hand reached down and took mine.

"Are you okay to stand up?" he asked.

I nodded and let him pull me to my feet. Everything around was sharp and crisp—I took in every detail but I couldn't connect anymore than if I were trapped in a snow globe.

My knees buckled and I slipped down the front of his jacket. The muscles underneath were strong. I wanted to slide my hand under his shirt when he pulled me against him and shuttled me rock-star style through a crowd of t-shirts. A turquoise Alice in Wonderland top in front of me read "If you chase rabbits, you'll end up having tea with the Mad Hatter."

That was me. Falling into a hole. We walked past a white gate and into a building. The door clicked, locking out all sound except a tiny ringing in my ears. The black blazer ushered me down a Pluto-yellow hallway to a women's room door.

"I'm Colin Donnelly, Park Director."

I placed my hand back into his and still had room for four more hands. He paused and stared at my face. I watched him watch me. I guessed he was a few years older. His face held a few lines at his eyes and he twisted his expression, deciding if I was about to faint again. His hair was jet black, like if Snow White had a son.

I didn't realize Colin had my bag until he held it out to me. "I'm sure you'll want to freshen up. Anyway, I'll be down the hall, second door on the right."

Why is everyone telling me to clean up?

The unrecognizable face that met me in the mirror answered that question. Mascara ran down one side of my face in a root beer drip with a line of confetti. A multi-colored tear. Except, I didn't cry. Not in almost ten years.

I twisted the Mickey's hand-shaped faucet and let the water run warm. I washed off the smudged makeup I'd applied this morning when I still looked like Michael's wife and watched the colors swirl down the drain with pieces of confetti. I'd been so excited about coming to the park; I hadn't given my hair and makeup the special attention Michael liked. And I'd spent so much time on the park website I hadn't done any of my ironing. My shirt was a crumpled mess.

I dug through my large bag and pulled out the foundation and shadows Michael had chosen from the make-up counter. My shaking hands bobbled the kit and it slipped out of my grasp and shattered on the white floor tiles into a pile of his favorite colors. I dropped to my knees grabbing at bits and pieces that disintegrated at my touch.

A wet smudge of color covered the back of my hand when I wiped my cheek. My stomach muscles clenched and my vision blurred. "I don't cry." Tears upset Michael.

A loud sob burst through so strong that the sound scared me into a case of hiccups and full hysteria.

I wasn't sure how long I sat there on that bathroom floor crying. A tingling pain in the leg I'd been sitting on caused me to shift. When I saw that the cold tile floors had left an indentation on my calf that resembled fishnet stockings, I laughed. A cracking, runny nose of a laugh that took me back to the day I lost my parents.

"Your parents are dead," Michael had said, one hand holding the white courtesy phone, the other our boarding passes. "An accident."

"No way," I'd cackled, at the cruel joke. "Give me the phone."

"What's going on?" I'd asked, ready to chew someone out.

"It's true dear," Michael's mom had said. "They're gone. Don't worry. I'll be your mother now."

That was the first time the tiny sparkles of light twinkled at the corners of my eyes. It was odd how the light came before the darkness.

I'd fainted again at the mortuary when Mother Gunderson, as she'd insisted I call her, showed me the matching caskets she'd picked out.

"Aren't they lovely?" She'd waved an arm across the shiny, faux-wood surface, pointing out the brass knobs like game show prizes. "I'm sure they'd appreciate these."

I'd pictured Dad climbing inside. "Well the outside is okay," he'd say, "but this cushion is hard as a rock."

That was when I'd hit the floor.

So smart. So bright. I thought I'd talked Michael into leaving me alone at the park but all the while he'd set me up as his alibi. I dumped the ruined kit into the trash, dried off my face and brushed the shoulder length mess out. The familiar strokes against my scalp were calming. I thought back to the beginning with Michael.

A sophomore theater arts major, I'd been elected to host the new residents game night and Michael had just moved into my dorm. He was on academic probation from his freshman year of partying while living in a fraternity house.

After an evening of ice-breaker games where I'd caught him watching me several times, he'd walked up and introduced himself. "Your hair is so pretty," he'd said, twirling my long blond hair around his finger. "I bet it looks great up."

I'd just come out of my ugly duckling stage where most of my high school years were spent fighting pimples and waiting to bloom. My new stage was filled with covering up my D cups which were precariously attached to my thin build like an anatomically correct Miss Shoestring Potato Head. I'd thought my personality was still my best asset. But Michael loved everything about me. I'd sucked up Michael's praise, hungry for more. He was my Prince Charming—sweeping me away from my inadequate self perception.

He'd complimented my way with people. "You are the most caring, tender person I've ever met," Michael had said on our first date. "You should go into nursing. That's what all the women in my family did."

By the end of the year he slept over anytime my roommate was with her boyfriend and I'd happily started over in the nursing department, even though it had meant beginning a new set of general education requirements.

Michael's mother loved me. I was just what she'd wanted to settle her son down, she'd said. She had called regularly to make sure I watched that he did his homework, attended classes and stayed out of the frat house. She had confided that if he didn't step it up that year, they would pull the financial plug. I had helped keep him in school. Near me.

I didn't think I was one of those women who would take on the blame for their husband's infidelity. But when I dared to look back into the bathroom mirror, it was easy to see why Michael was with someone as young and fresh as Jessica. There was a big difference between twenty-two and three days from thirty.

I wished it hadn't happened here. I needed to get home, pack and leave before he returned. I couldn't face him, knowing I hadn't been woman or wife enough. Not in a million years.

Chapter 3

I barreled toward the building exit and straight into a round, white-haired woman short enough to make my five-foot-two inches feel tall. I veered around her to make my escape, but "do si do'ed" to the right as she linked our elbows and I faced the hallway again.

"Excuse me," I released my arm and tried to remember why she looked familiar.

"I've been waiting for you. I'm Felicity Centeno, VIP Host Manager," she said. "You've been in there a long time. Are you okay?"

"I guess so." She didn't believe me by the way she patted my arm, a golden World's Greatest Gramma charm dangled around her wrist.

"I'm sure it's a lot to take in. First of all, congratulations," she led me down the hall and her voice took on a tone used to calm either an unhappy two-year-old or a mental patient. "I'm so happy for you. I'll help you through the paperwork and be your guide while you're here at the park."

Conscious of my red eyes and still shaking hands, I tried to sound rational. *Small talk.*

"Aren't you the lady I saw talking to my husband's boss?" I stuttered over the word husband. I wouldn't have one for much longer.

"Yes and I was also lucky enough to be right behind you when you won the prize," she gave my arm a squeeze. "I could tell when you were helping that boy this morning that you know this park. Do you come often?"

"When I was growing up," I nodded. "Sleeping Beauty's Castle was my mom's favorite place on Earth. But I haven't been since I married."

Felicity knocked on a door, second from the right. A deep voice answered. "Come in."

Colin sat at an enormous dark wood structure that would have been imposing if it weren't surrounded by a collection of Disney memorabilia that screamed welcome.

His hair curled around the edges of his ears signaling he was due for a haircut. He had a nice smile when he turned to talk to Felicity, but frowned when he looked at my face. *How bad do I look today?*

He took a lap around the desk, his arm outstretched. "Please have a seat." He motioned to a small round table mysteriously held up by two bright yellow legs that sat in large white shoes with bows—Daisy Duck's feet.

Once in grade school I played a game where you looked at a tray full of items for one minute, then without looking at it again, you tried to write down everything that was on the tray. I never remembered more than four or five items. But though the bubble erected around me kept everything inside fuzzy, every item in the room was sharp and clear—imprinting in my mind in a way that I would remember forever.

Trying to forget my moment of lust when I'd first touched Colin, I ignored him—my attention pulled to the bookshelves covered in photos of Disney celebrities—Mickey, Minnie, Goofy and Donald— heads of state, each one shaking the hand or with an arm around a uniformed Disney employee. They were all of Colin.

I couldn't imagine such a history. I'd bounced through schools and programs too much in the last years to make or keep any friends. My parents wouldn't like my life. They would blame Michael. Again.

"But you're so talented," Mom had said when I'd first switched majors. "You were the lead in all your school plays. You have something special."

"You have to say that, you're my mom. Michael thinks I should have a real career in nursing. And I do love helping people."

"But what do you think?" Dad had asked. "So far all I've heard is his opinion."

"I agree with Michael." Of course I had. "I'll miss theater but it's not like I was any good."

Dad was about to explode when Mom stepped in.

"That's fine dear. If this is what you'd like to do we're behind you," she had stared Dad down. "Right honey?"

"Of course," he'd slid back into his arm chair and shielded his face with the paper he'd already finished reading. "I was going to have my friends come to all your productions. Guess I'll make sure they all come to you for blood pressure checks and prostate exams."

The photo of Mickey with Colin in the white uniform of a street sweeper must have been taken when he was a teenager, but it was grainy and hard to make out for sure. He had the same broad shoulders, but was

21

thinner in build. The arms and chest grew as the photos moved from left to right and his uniforms changed from Jungle Boat captain to his first photo in a suit.

Mom had kept the photos she'd taken of me with Mickey in a row like this on the living room mantle.

"Mickey will always be the same," Mom's voice bounced on the walls of my bubble as the memory of having Mom point her camera at me and Mickey filled my mind, "and you'll grow and change. It's important to have constants in your life."

I'd saved all the photos in the attic, hidden with the rest of my parents' items which Michael never wanted to see again. He was always a big fan of purging, even before the home shows made it popular. Although, it was my things he had an urge to purge. The shelves that once celebrated my growth now held his fraternity ping pong trophies, employee-of-the-month plaques and model airplanes.

A tiny wind-up Minnie dressed in a wedding gown caught my attention and drew me back to the worst day of my life.

"He's not the right man for you," Dad had said when we stood at the back of the church, ready to walk me down the aisle. "I've left my car outside with the keys in the ignition. I'll fake a heart attack and you run like crazy away from this man. Please Mini, run."

"You're wrong," I'd said. "Why can't you just be happy for us?"

"I was afraid you'd say that. So I've saved our house for you. If I died today, at least I know you'll always have a home."

I'd still taken his arm and walked down the aisle smiling—at Michael. The first time I turned to look at my parents as a married woman I saw tears in both their eyes. Knowing they weren't tears of happiness had pissed me off. After all the years of unconditional love why had they chosen my wedding day to be stupid?

Mom had hugged me in the hallway. "Be happy dear. We're always here for you."

"That's not what Dad said," I had pouted.

"He wants to protect you. We just don't like the way Michael's changing you."

"Maybe I do."

Dad and Mom had left after the cake was cut. I'd wanted to tell them that I'd prove Michael was the right man for me. But I'd never seen them again.

"Dear, Colin is speaking to you," Felicity touched my arm. I turned to face him, but I was still thinking of Dad.

"We'll need some identification and we don't even know your name," Colin said.

I set the toy back on his desk. "Mini."

"Good Lord," he said, "she thinks she's Minnie Mouse."

I opened my bag and dug out my wallet, handing my license to Felicity. "Mini, as in short for Margaret," I sighed. "No relation to the mouse."

"We have a few minutes to go over the paperwork for your prize," Colin said. "Then the camera crew will be here and we'll have the official award ceremony."

"Camera crew?" I rubbed at my hair. Everything about today connected to how bad I looked.

"It's the biggest prize we've awarded in Disneyland's history," Colin added. "Your first decision is if you'd like your stay to begin now or at another date more convenient for you."

"Stay?" I wound up the Daisy Duck and watched her hop across the desk. *Will I stay with Michael? Will I get my family?*

"Uh Felicity, can I speak to you in the hallway?" Colin asked. "We'll be just a moment."

Their muffled voices were loud enough to hear through the door.

"Felicity," Colin's voice boomed, "I'm wondering if we should have the doctor check her out before we proceed. She could have hit her head harder than we thought when she fainted. She is about to sign a contract after all."

The director believed I was a complete idiot. I would have been offended, but fainting had put a question mark on my mental prowess. I didn't want to see a doctor. I needed to get my things and run.

"She might be the one," Felicity defended.

"Now that I want to see—particularly since you've known her all of ten minutes," Colin laughed. "I swear, you believe in everyone."

"You haven't trusted anyone since you-know-what. It's time Colin."

"Are we talking about work or my personal life?" he growled.

"Work is your personal life," she said. "After all, I am a professional fairy godmother."

"Okay," he said. "The usual bet?"

"I'm still trying."

I couldn't make out the rest of the conversation because a shiny red Mickey Mouse spinning top drew me away to the corner and happier memories. I sat on the floor spinning it around the low carpet and thinking of Mom and Dad when Colin and Felicity returned and the sound of Colin's laughter erupted as he said, "I am so going to win!"

Chapter 4

"Mini," Felicity reached down for my hand and helped me up. "Part of your prize is a two-night stay in Sleeping Beauty's Castle. Did you have something or someone to go home to? Something planned that will keep you from staying at the park the next two nights?"

Yes! Fly to Vegas and confront Michael. My shoulders shook and laughter threatened to erupt. I'd never told him that French twists gave me a headache. Catching him cheating was not something I was going to admit.

I slapped my hand over my mouth and snorted. "No. I'm free." *Free to believe I'm going absolutely crazy.*

"How about we have you sign just the press release at this time, then later when things settle down a bit, you can make decisions on the rest of your prize?" Felicity's hand was warm on my shoulder. "Would you like to spend a couple of nights in Sleeping Beauty's Castle dear?"

"The Castle is where all the dreams come true." Mom's voice returned and I pictured her tossing a coin into Snow White's wishing well at the Castle base. I nodded to Felicity.

"Then read this and sign here," she handed me a tall skinny Goofy-shaped pen, "and we'll get you started."

I squinted and stared at the contract in front of me,

but all I saw was Michael kissing Jessica. I shook my head to clear it, but grew dizzy. "Where do I sign?"

"Don't you want to read it through?"

"Not really," I signed the spot near Felicity's finger. *Disneyland had never given me any reason to distrust.*

"Let me read the high points to you to consider for later." Felicity ran down a lengthy list. "The first part of the prize includes unlimited access to all Disney parks for the rest of your life, the stay at the Castle and a ten-thousand dollar shopping spree. This is all non-transferrable."

She lost me at shopping and my mind wandered back to Michael. I sucked at selecting anything. Michael picked out clothes for me to try on that he thought worked best. It always took me so long and time was money, right?

Felicity's voice droned on. Something about keys, prizes, room service—

"Food?" *Did I eat anything today?*

"Yes, of course. You'll be wearing a badge that will allow you immediate access to every ride and concession at Disneyland. And of course if you're married, your husband and children are included."

"No kids," I sighed again. I wasn't sure I'd ever sighed before, but I liked it. Exhaling pain and then breathing in all the good Disneyland air. "My husband's out of town."

"And your parents? Do you hear from them often?"

Only in my head. "No. They died in a car accident on their way home from my wedding."

Colin choked like he had something scratchy stuck in his throat. His attractiveness waned.

"Can you back up?" My stomach growled. "Was there something about food?"

"Certainly," she said. "What would you like?"

My hair still smelled and made me thirsty. "A corn dog and root beer."

Felicity pulled her phone out, pressed one digit and repeated my order, naming me Sleeping Beauty. "That's your call sign for the crew to know that you need something. Mustard or ketchup?"

"Mustard." Michael never asked. He always bought ketchup because that was what he liked.

She repeated my order into the phone. "So if you'll sign here agreeing to be followed by a camera crew as part of our publicity, then we can get right to things."

"Michael complains I live in a different reality," I said. "Now I'll have my own show."

"Not exactly, but I do understand your husband," Colin snorted. Felicity glared at him. She believed in me for some reason. Anyone who knew me would back Colin.

Felicity smiled. "We'll start the filming once we leave this building and then keep rolling off and on through your parade."

"My parade?"

"You'll be queen of the four-thirty parade on the day after tomorrow. There will be a costume fitting and then a quick rehearsal before the parade. We'll need to do some taping today and then again tomorrow afternoon. The rest of your stay you'll be free to do whatever you want."

Michael would freak—his wife belonged in the background. But I'd signed the publicity release because I didn't like my husband kissing other women.

I wouldn't be here for the parade anyway. I'd be long gone. My destination was still fuzzy. I traded the pen for a corn dog the instant it arrived.

"There's more," Felicity continued. "The second part of the prize is an annual vacation, every year for life through Disney Travel to all locations including Hong Kong, Tokyo and the many cruise destinations. This part has a cash-out clause of one-hundred thousand. Of course it's worth much more."

A tiny piece of cornbread combined with the value of the prize and started me coughing for a minute. When the hacking stopped, Felicity continued to talk about contract stuff. But I went deaf again to hear my parents while I concentrated on crunching through the mustard-coated sensation, cooling off my mouth with slugs of icy root beer in a purple cup dotted with faces of Mickey.

"Aren't these the greatest?" Dad asked. He'd always eat at least two.

Colin pulled Felicity aside and spoke loud enough to make it through. "She's attractive enough, but is she okay you know...for the cameras?" He tapped a finger to his forehead.

"She's overwhelmed."

"I'll back you as far as I can, but I have to think of the implications if things go...South shall we say?" They spoke as if I wasn't there. I wasn't.

"Everything's going to be perfect."

"Okay Felicity, I'll trust you." I watched him sign his name with large open letters. Michael's writing was pinched. 'E. Colin Donnelly.'

"What does the E. stand for?" I asked.

The edges of his mouth turned down further than I thought possible. "Don't ask, don't tell."

"Are you ready dear?" Felicity touched my arm and I tingled. "I'll be with you all the time if you'd like. I can help make all your wishes come true."

"My own fairy godmother?" My attention moved to another shelf.

"Candy from a baby…" Colin chuckled.

"I bet I know your favorite," Dad's voice comforted me. I pictured him selecting a pink parasol from a cart and handing it to me. "You always loved pink."

"Miss. Miss." Colin's voice interrupted again. I flicked my fingers at my ears trying to block him out and strained to hear Mom and Dad. I wanted a world filled with their voices before my life screwed itself up.

"Miss, you should see our doctor. Look at her Felicity. She can't even hear me."

My anger and his persistence drowned my parent's voices. I was now standing in the present. Michael was cheating on me. The only voices I wanted to hear had been silenced by this man who told me I was crazy.

Ok, so I never graduated college. I'm not so bright. But I'm kind to old people and animals and I'd never speak to someone like he was.

"You know it's not nice to talk about people like they aren't there," I said. "Don't do it again." Colin's mouth hung open and a rush of power filled me. I could shut up a big man and I liked it.

"Come along Mini," Felicity took my arm again and tried to squelch a smile. "Let's see if we can make your dreams come true."

If a dream was a wish your heart makes when you're fast asleep, I should have a boatload—I'd been asleep

31

for years. But as we walked down the hallway, I couldn't conjure up a single wish. If I'd wished for children, Michael would be unhappy. If I wished for fulfillment, what would that mean?

I didn't know my own dreams. But I knew Michael's in detail. He'd always wanted to be a commercial jet pilot flying the Pacific route with regular stops in Hawaii, Singapore, Vietnam and China. During his layovers he wanted to study the local area with special interest in any place or anyone having been involved in major wars.

He had been talking about it for ages. I once made the mistake of asking why he studied business and not aeronautics, geography or history.

"My dad's idea of a successful man is himself," Michael had declared. "He wants me to be him. Study business, get in on the ground floor somewhere, earn your dues, marry someone like Mom and spend any free time on the golf course—a hobby that combines physical exercise with excellent opportunities to combine business with pleasure. He's even got me a job with his friend at toy factory to get my foot in the door."

"But what about what you want? My parents would never put their ideas of what I should be on me. They've always supported whatever I've wanted to do."

"My parents aren't bad," he'd defended.

"I didn't mean they were," I'd backpedaled. "Just that if you want to be a pilot, you should be."

"It's not that easy. I'd have to join the Air Force to get enough hours to fly commercial jets."

"That's a big decision," I'd said. "But at least we're not at war anywhere right now."

"Yeah, too bad. Would you worry about me?"

"Of course. But I'd support whatever you need to be happy."

"Talking to you makes me almost believe I could do it."

A rampant case of large red pimples held my self esteem at a low point until I burst through my senior year with a clear face and lead in the school musical. Up to that point, my parents were the sole members of my fan club.

Theater was great. Any type of positive attention outside of my house was refreshing. I had always thought my parents were just being kind to be nice.

It wasn't until Michael was attracted to me that I thought of myself as a woman. He loved my hair, my way with others and the feel of my breasts when I was excited.

Chapter 5

Cheers from a large crowd filled the quiet hallway when Felicity opened the white gate. Every speck of confetti had disappeared—a miracle of Disney cleaning crews—replaced with a long red carpet bordered with dozens of balloons and hundreds of eyes. All looking at me.

"I can't do this," I squeaked and ducked back into the safety of the building.

"I knew it," Colin barked. "I'll go make the announcement without her."

"Wait!" My brain told me to exit stage left, but an alien attitude was building inside me. I didn't want him to win. "Let's go."

I pasted a smile on my face and tried not to think of the last time I walked down an aisle as we made our way to the base of the steps of the Main Train Station. Balloons in the shape of the Castle were being handed out to children.

Colin motioned for me to wait on the steps. I hoped the look I gave him passed as a sneer as he went to the microphone.

"We have wonderful news," he began. "For the first time in Disneyland history we are about to unlock the Castle. Never since Walt Disney first dreamed of this park in 1936 has anyone imagined how wonderful this award would be."

Blah, blah, blah. All I heard from him was 'I love the sound of my own voice.'

I smiled at a little girl standing next to me. She wasn't impressed by my win. She couldn't take her eyes off the Minnie Mouse dress another girl wore.

She had the same straight hair I always had but in pigtails. A mirror image of myself as a girl. Her mother wore her same straight hair in a ponytail. Michael thought pony tails were juvenile. But no one wore French twists anymore. Only me and Michael's mom.

The little girl reached for the Minnie Mouse costume. "Mommy, can I have one?" she asked.

"I'm sorry Sarah, but I used all I had to get us in here for your birthday," the mom whispered and patted Sarah's head. "Maybe next year baby."

"And now I have the extreme pleasure to introduce our Grand Prize winner Mini Gunderson," Colin said. *What a crock. He's not pleased by me at all.*

Felicity held my elbow and steered me to the podium and up three steps to a stage where Mickey waited. I ignored Colin and went straight into Mickey's arms. There it was. The wonderful scent of new plastic toys—soft and comforting. Tears fell and Felicity pulled me out of the embrace.

Holding Mickey Mouse's gloved hand I turned to face the crowd, brushing away a new wave of tears. So many people smiling . . . at me.

Mickey tapped me on the shoulder and pointed to Colin. "To our Grand Prize winner," Colin announced, "Mickey wants to extend the key that will unlock the Castle."

Mickey held out a lanyard with a key-shaped tag hanging on it that held my photo—taken the instant I had won and before my eyes had rolled back into my head. To compare my look to a deer in the headlights would have been an insult to Bambi. I put down my head and was crowned by Mickey. The crowd roared and I waved.

"Would you like to say a few words?" Colin asked. *He thinks I'm an idiot.* He shook his head a bit, hoping I would say no. He wanted control over me. Just like Michael. I looked down at the little girl. Someone else should have a day to remember. I took the microphone for the first time since Michael told me I had no real talent for the stage.

"I want to say thank you to Disneyland and my guide Felicity. And I know Mickey wants to wish a special Happy Birthday to Sarah," I pointed down to her and Mickey blew a kiss. Sarah beamed. Her mother smiled so hard, tears squeezing out of her eyes. "Everyone should have a special birthday."

I searched the area and spied a little girl's dream. "I'd like to invite all the birthday girls with me to the princess shop and let's all get dressed up to celebrate my prize! My treat." Cheers roared from the crowd while I was bustled off the stage between Felicity and Colin. I motioned for Sarah to catch up.

Colin went straight to the register to speak with the clerk. Her smile was regulation Disney. She made a timid nod to her boss and he explained what was about to happen. I moved out of the way for three little girls and their mom.

"Thank you so much," the woman said, and I stepped back to allow another group into the store. I saw Sarah and her mom were already at the register with the Minnie Mouse dress. Her smile was enough for me. I waited for the flow of girls entering the store to thin so I could move outside. But it didn't lighten up. The crowd grew thicker, pushing me further into the store.

Pressed against the room capacity sign on the back wall I knew I'd underestimated the number of little girls celebrating a birthday and the possible sound level generated by tiny bodies. Squeals bounced off the walls of the small shop as mothers and daughters emptied the racks of dresses in a sequined frenzy.

Searching for a vantage point, I crawled up onto a treasure chest display, using a princess-dressed mannequin on my left for balance. Both doors were blocked by girls of all sizes and a long line pressed against the check-out counter where piles of dotted, tulle and satin costumes were building.

Colin stood beside the clerk, bagging the dresses she rang up. Up to his ears in Snow White costumes, his eyes met mine. His mouth widened into an O as I sunk into the collapsing chest. I tightened my grip on the mannequin's silky brown tresses with my left hand and grabbed at a metal bracket holding baby dresses with my right.

The cracking sound of the bracket screws popping out of the wall caught the attention of the entire noisy room. Every eye turned to watch when my support gave away and I landed on my butt in a rain of ruffles and lace—still clutching the metal bar and a long wig.

My feet were trapped inside the paper mache chest, making crawling out impossible, so I curled up and waited for security to arrive. Thirty minutes and four thousand Disney dollars later I was ushered out over empty hangers and toppled racks. I was back in the safe room, but not safe from Colin.

"So you can speak," Colin growled. "If you are going to start any other riots, could you give me a little notice? That shop was between a shift change and two employees hadn't shown up yet."

I would have been scared, but the bridge of his nose was dusted in green Tinker Bell glitter.

Chapter 6

My first riot. Granted, no televisions were looted and the political balance of the state of California remained the same. But I had overworked the poor clerk and inconvenienced Colin.

It was time to go, but Felicity didn't agree.

"Let's go do some shopping of our own," Felicity said. She pulled me down the back corridor toward the store. I hated shopping, but I had been bad and needed to be punished.

Three Main Street stores later the only purchase I'd made was a bag of sour gumdrops. I popped the last one in my mouth by the time I ground to a halt in front of a display of model airplanes.

Last year when Michael had taken our old car to a sale lot he'd come home with a plane. Pieces, anyway. In the garage rests the body of a Cessna. The wings are in storage and he spends time reading through books on how to rebuild a plane engine. That was another secret I kept for him.

A large tarp covers the fuselage in case his dad stops by. But there was no fear of his Dad seeing. The old man always walked straight through the house to the putting green.

Michael doesn't know I can hear him from the adjoining laundry room, when he sits in the pilot's seat and talks to an imaginary radio tower.

41

"Whiskey Romeo One Blue Leader, this is the Blue Bomber requesting clearance for takeoff."

He'd make the same sounds during a long soak in the bath while emptying my bubble jar—practicing flying tiny plastic planes through cloudy bubble formations.

"Not seeing anything you want?" Felicity pulled me back.

"It's not that." I didn't want to admit Michael usually did my shopping. "You pick out something for me. I'm the most indecisive person ever. I never know what I want."

"Oh no, you should select your favorites," Felicity pulled me to a rack of dresses. "You'll need a few things for the next couple of days since you're not going home."

"Okay." I tried to picture how much stuff would fit in the car. Michael's car. I didn't have one of my own. *How do I move out? All I could carry?* And then Michael would get half of the house. The home Dad had tried to save for me.

"Go ahead, choose whatever you want. It's on the park." Felicity smiled and I lifted at least one corner of my mouth in return. I didn't want to tell her the truth. The more I told her, the worse I'd look.

In the room full of color, there was nothing Michael would want. Michael wanted Jessica. I picked up a blue Winnie the Pooh umbrella and swung it back and forth as I walked through the aisle. I dressed like Jessica when we first met. Young, fresh and a little sexy maybe.

By now, Michael had picked out every item in my closet. He had changed me to what he wanted. Or had changed me into what he didn't want.

"I see you've found a few things," Felicity interrupted my thoughts.

"Huh?" I didn't remember picking up the collection of items. An antenna ball shaped like a super Mickey flying through the sky for the car I didn't have, a pair of high-heeled slippers two sizes too small and a refrigerator magnet of Goofy rushing for a touchdown.

"That's a good start," Felicity took the items from me and nodded to the racks of clothes. "You'll need a few things to wear."

Acid built up in my stomach from a combination of too much sour candy and a fear of choice.

I had no idea what I wanted—what to wear or to do with my life. I grabbed three items and looked for an escape route. "Is there a dressing room?"

"Right over there," Felicity pointed.

"I'll meet you back here." I tucked myself into the stall and waited for a chance to slip out unnoticed. After five minutes passed, I cracked open the door.

"Did you like any of them?" Felicity waited two steps outside the door with an armful of clothes.

"Uh, no."

"Then try these," the weight of the pile of spring colored dresses added to the pressure in my heart. "Let me see the red one on you."

Out of options, I wrapped the sundress around and secured the row of tiny buttons, tight over my mammoth breasts. Avoiding my eyes in the mirror in the event the sight would restart the tears, I stepped out to show Felicity the dress.

"You have to keep that. It's lovely. Why not wear it to the parade? Pick out some pajamas," she pulled off the tag and lured me over to racks of pink flannel and filmy fabrics. I picked out my size, ready to leave. "And some slippers and a tooth brush."

She continued to pull me through the store, forcing me to choose from the huge variety of items until tears threatened to drop down my face. I was afraid that once I started looking at all that was possible, I wouldn't be able to leave.

"Can we do something else?" I asked Felicity after the items were bagged. "I'm worn out from the Princess snafu."

"Certainly. How about I select a few things for you later and send them to your room. If you don't like them, we can always swap them out." Felicity glanced at her Classic Mickey watch and led me out to the sidewalk. "It's time for the parade. We have a special front row seat ready for you."

"I love watching the parade," Mom's voice giggled.

"Me too," I said aloud.

"What?" Felicity asked.

"Uh, I love parades."

Mom and Dad would always pick out a spot on the curb early then save it for me while one of them took me on all the rides—with lines shortened as crowds gathered for the parade.

I turned down Felicity's offer to have my pants and shirt sent to the Castle and tucked them into my purse, expanded to capacity.

Felicity pulled me through the sea of people and my mind waffled between sadness, disbelief and jealousy.

How did Jessica deserve the good kisses? Youth? Beauty? Her own getaway car?

Felicity held my arm and we weaved around the crowds lined up to watch the parade so I couldn't make a break for it. At the roped edge near the head of Main Street, a yellow-shirted employee lifted the barricade and waved me toward my seat—a purple velvet-covered throne topped with a carved wooden head of Mickey Mouse.

On the parade side of the blockade, the floats would come straight at me. I wanted to laugh and cry on the best and worst day in my life.

I climbed the matching stepstool up into the soft seat which sat high enough for a vantage point of the entire Main Street. I sighed as the velvet seat took me off my feet for a moment. By the large clock in front of me it wasn't even noon yet and I was ready to climb into bed for a nap. All I needed was a half hour, or maybe lifetime, under the covers.

Tears seeped to the brim of my eyes again and I thought of Dad running for our snacks and Mom guarding over his seat.

"The floats will turn in front of you and then exit into the back lot," Felicity said. "Please stay seated until the parade is over and I'll be here to escort you back."

I forced a small nod to make the lie not so big. I'd be gone before she returned.

"Would you like anything to eat?" Felicity asked.

"I don't want you to go to any trouble." Although it would give me a chance to leave without explanation. "Maybe some popcorn?"

I stood and waited for her to disappear into the crowd, then noticed a small boy in red overalls straining against his mother's hand to see down the street at the advancing parade. The mother used her free hand to soothe a small baby in the stroller with a pacifier.

Pangs of jealousy stabbed at me. I was so used to them, they almost didn't hurt. I'd wanted children for years, but Michael wanted to wait. He'd wanted to enjoy his youth. Now I was still motherless, but he had a child. A twenty-two year old with beautiful hair and outrageous high-heeled shoes and I have what? A plan to run away to nowhere.

A giant nodding red lady bug made her way down the route when my phone rang.

Michael. I fumbled through my purse to find the phone with shaking hands and a racing heart. *He's calling to tell me he's not coming back.*

"Hello?" I couldn't summon up the strength for any other words. I braced myself for the coming end of my reality.

"What's your 10-20? Has Chris seen you yet?"

"What?" *Oh yeah, my location.*

"Have you seen Chris? Is my secret safe?"

"Not yet," my legs buckled and I sat back down. "Did you want to tell me anything?"

"Like what?" he sighed. "You sound very strange babe. After you see Chris maybe you should go home and get some rest. "

"Home?"

"Yes Margaret, our home. I know you don't like to lie, but don't let it make you crazy. Relax."

Relax? How exactly am I supposed to do this?
"There's nothing else you called to tell me?"

46

"What else is there? I'll be home in a few days and it will be as if this never happened. Help me out today and keep my secret."

Is it a one-time thing? Is he getting it out of his system with plans to go on like nothing happened? A male-aging crisis? I nodded into the phone. Parade music trumpeted out the speakers above me. "I'll keep your secret."

"I can't hear you above the noise. I'm hanging up."

"I'll never tell." I said to the click of his phone. Could I go on as if nothing happened—living a secret life in my parent's home? Was it my only chance for a family? I sunk back into my throne. The day after tomorrow, I would be entering a new age category. Statistics of terrorist attacks versus finding new love spun in my head when Felicity arrived with a box of popcorn.

"Are you all right?" she asked. "You've lost all the color in your face."

"I'm fine." Why did I always say fine? Even when I had the swine flu, a high fever and couldn't hold down water I'd told the doctor "fine."

He wants to keep his secret from Jessica's dad. That must mean it's going to end. He's not going to leave me. He's coming back to me. He'll return with his secret and I'll keep my dream of finally having a family again.

"Do you need something else?" Felicity asked. "Perhaps a drink?"

"Uh, yeah." My mother-in-law drank gin and tonics between five and six o'clock every day. They smelled horrible, but they had a positive effect on her attitude. I wanted one or four of them. I was tired of my own lameness and I had the world on my mind.

"Let me get you another root beer. That should perk you up," she said. It wasn't what I was thinking about, but it would have to do.

Michael said he was coming home. If I kept his secret then everything would return to the way it was. Floats moved straight at me in perfect lines, spaced at timed intervals that allowed dancers and musicians between. I had the best seat in the house. I had something so many wanted but Michael would never understand.

I'd like to pretend for a few hours that my life hadn't been dumped upside down. I would keep Michael's secret. And I would keep one of my own. One day. Today. I would stay at Disneyland until the last guest leaves and pretend to be happy. I would have my secret day to figure something out.

Pumba and Timon chased bugs around a float of the Lion King and I watched the toddler in the overalls again. His voice increased as he pulled against his mom's hand. He drew her inches closer to the rope set up to hold the crowd back from the parade. His curly brown hair shone with golden highlights.

The theme music softened, and then changed. The next float was the Disney Princess castle replica with several pairs of royal couples from Eric and Ariel to Belle and the Beast dancing the perimeter in choreographed movements to a lilting waltz. Sleeping Beauty and Prince Charming twirled on top. Their sequins glistened bright in the midday sun.

"Anything else?" Felicity asked. I hadn't realized she'd returned with the soda.

48

"Toffee?" Dad always bought toffee.

"No problem," she said and was off again.

The toddler squealed and grabbed my attention. The Princess float rounded the corner in front of me as the toddler broke free of his mother's hand and charged the enormous vehicle.

I flung the food and dove off the throne.

Before I hit the pavement the startled face of the child froze—held back by a toddler harness, the strap anchored to his mom's wrist.

"Smack!" The sound of a wrong decision hitting the ground was never pretty—like when I was ten and tried to ride myself on the handlebar of my blue Stingray.

Having tackled myself and lost I popped up to act like nothing happened but pain from my head and knee dropped me back down.

A squealing sound pierced my ears and a ruffle of the float skirt brushed my face. I focused ahead as the blurry vision cleared and a set of double tires rolled toward my nose.

I was pulled up into strong arms as the loud crunching sound of two floats colliding sent a sigh through the crowd. I focused on a face. Prince Charming?

"Great dream." I drawled or maybe drooled against his blue velvet tunic and I touched the lump that used to be my head. The asphalt was hard today. "Did I knock you off the float or can you fly?"

The Prince smiled, teeth sparkling, lips wet and kissable. Blue eyes shining. "Are you all right?" he asked. I wrapped my arms around his neck, ready to show him how all right I was when Colin pulled my arms free and set me upright.

49

"Your dress," Colin pointed to the gaping front of my unbuttoned top. He held me by one arm, the other activating his ear piece radio while he blocked my front. I blushed. The Prince smiled. I grabbed at the buttons and struggled to cover up my bra, while at the same time wishing I hadn't picked out the beige serviceable model this morning.

"Thank you," Colin dismissed the Prince. "Are you a lunatic?" he whispered to me, then said into the radio "Hold up the back. Collision in front." I watched the Prince's well-toned butt ripple under his white tights. He took Sleeping Beauty's hand and continued their waltz amidst the Dixieland band that had run out of room when the two floats buckled together.

"That float weighs tons," Colin lowered me to the curb. "You could have been killed."

"The little boy…" I yelled as the tuba player, squeezed out of space, blared above me. "He was going to be crushed by the float."

"Boy?" Colin sucked in air as if he was about to submerge, then slipped under the edge of the float.

Colin resurfaced from the empty sub-float in a filthy suit with lips pierced tight enough to hold back the flow of words his squinted eyes wanted to say to me.

"I just turned my back," Felicity said as she moved between us. She held one arm and Colin the other as they lifted and ushered me back to first aid, past the Prince's float, limping into the backlot.

"Red overalls…" I mumbled. "He was going to be hurt. I tried to help."

"I know Mini." Felicity patted my hand—the one part of me that didn't hurt—her softly wrinkled skin silky to the touch. "Your heart was in the right place, but your body wasn't. Let's get you checked out at first aid, then maybe a rest."

"Keep an eye on her," Colin growled. "I've got to talk to the film crew about some editing!" He let go of my arm as we entered the large white building and the twinkling lights returned to the corners of my eyes as I sunk.

Chapter 7

The Little Mermaid band aid on my knee wasn't big enough to disappear under.

"Sit and stay," Colin said through a tight smile. He planted me on a bench in front of a small waterfall surrounded by statues of Snow White and the Seven Dwarves. Snow had run into the woods to escape persecution. I wished I could hide out here and figure out what to do.

Colin listened to something through his ear piece. "Don't move." His wide shoulders had risen inches in tension since I'd met him this morning. He looked back at me as if torn between work and not trusting me on my own again.

I wasn't planning on moving. The embarrassment of two hours of observation at the first aid station was way too fresh.

I closed my eyes and searched for my happy place. My mind went straight to the Prince. And lust. Then I pictured Jessica with my Michael. I tried to shake her out of my head as the recorded soprano tones of Snow White rang out.

"Catch mommy," a tiny voice called behind me.

"Oops," the woman's voice said.

I will not turn.

"Dumbo!" The child screamed and cried with sugar induced, over stimulated gusto.

None of my business...none of my business....

The squealing wheel of a stroller screeched behind me.

"Excuse me" a voice said.

Damn.

I turned to find a young woman about seventeen-months pregnant. Her cheeks were pink with exertion, feet swelling over the sides of her flip flops. "Could you help me?" she begged over the sound of her screaming two-year-old. "Her stuffed Dumbo is in the wishing well and I can't quite reach it."

She patted her swollen mound and I resisted the urge to count the dwarf statues, to see which one she might have swallowed.

"Sure." *My name is Mini Gunderson and I have a compulsive need to help others and destroy Disneyland in the process.* At least this person asked for my help. That would be my defense later if needed. I saw Colin about fifty feet away, oblivious to me for once, thumb on his earpiece speaking into his radio.

I leaned over the stone walls of the small well, peering down. Dumbo's eyes looked up at me. He wished he hadn't left his magic feather in his other trunk, no doubt.

Fetch a doll. I can handle that.

I reached down to Dumbo, my fingertips brushing his head. But just my fingertips. I stood back up again.

The child cried louder. "Dumbo!"

"Oh, Baby, don't cry. She tried. The nice lady tried."

"I can do this," I just needed to slip into a phone booth, change into my cape and fly down. "I need a better angle." Stretching over the side again, I still couldn't quite reach, so I hiked myself up, leaned over, and snagged the elephant's nose, but it slipped out.

"Hang on. I'll get Dumbo this time." Using the sides of the well for leverage, I slid down far enough for my weight to be on my hands—one hand over Dumbo, my left on the wet swirling iron grill covering a pile of coins.

"Here you go!" My voice echoed from the small cave. I handed Dumbo up behind me and the child's crying switched off.

"Thank you so much," the woman said.

The blood rushing to my head pooled behind the black and blue knot from the parade. Pushing back to regain my balance, my wedding ring caught on the grillwork, pinching my finger. I pulled but couldn't free it—*crap!* "Uh, excuse me up there. Could I ask a favor?" I didn't want to start the child crying again so I used my 'everything's okay even though I'm stuck in a well' voice. "My ring is caught. Can you—"

"Oh sorry, sorry!" the woman said before I finished—and then she grabbed the back of my belt and yanked.

I screamed, in surprise and in pain at the sensation of my finger trying not be ripped from my hand. "No, no! Don't pull me up. My ring is stuck on the grill. Can you get someone?" I winced, knowing where this was going but also knowing that I was dizzier by the second. *Ah, Damn:* "There's a man in a blue blazer near the statue who can help. Can you get him, please?"

"Oh my, I'm sorry. It's all my fault! I'll be right back."

It was easy to see what Jessica had that I didn't. So far, Jessica wore high heels, graduated college, and didn't get stuck in wells. Jessica three, me zero.

The throb from the bump on my head matched the pulsing of my finger. I stared at my ring and remembered the day he'd surprised me with it.

Two days before graduation he planned to go to Tijuana with a friend, where they'd both get USAF tattoos and enlist, and then he'd break the news to his controlling parents after it was too late to stop him. After flight training, we'd be together.

He'd wanted me to drive him to T.J., but a night at a tattoo parlor drinking tequila wasn't my idea of fun.

The next morning he'd called from the police station for bail. DUI. No flight school. No Air Force. With that on his record, his dream was over. They'd never let him enlist, let alone become a pilot.

And then he took the permanent job at Chris' Toys.

The DUI was the first secret he asked me to keep for him. I owed it to him. If I'd driven him, his dream would have been intact.

The phone vibrated and rang in the back pocket of the shorts Felicity had bought me after I tore the dress under the float. The sound was probably drawing attention to my skyward pointing butt and the last of my dignity. I didn't want to talk to Michael. But if I didn't answer, I didn't know what he'd do. I always answered his calls. I grabbed for my pocket and managed to pull out my cell phone, using my mouth to open the flip top.

"Hello Michael," I squeaked.

"What did you do Margaret?" He sighed. The same voice Michael's father used. He expected me to answer.

"What do you mean?" Afraid I would tell him what I was doing. Scared I would admit I saw him with her.

"I can hear it in your voice. Don't worry. I've told you a million times that lying when you're trying to help someone is okay."

"It's not that. I, uh, just got off the tea cup ride." My first lie to Michael. Even as the bump on my head throbbed, it was easy to lie to my husband. He'd started it.

"I told you that makes you sick. You should know better."

"You're right Michael." *So many things make me sick.*

"I've reached my target and dropped my load." Why didn't he say he'd arrived at the hotel and unpacked? "Don't try to call me. I won't have my phone on. I wouldn't be able to hear it over the planes anyway. Have you seen Chris yet? I need you. You need to come through for me."

"Not yet." Of course from my vantage post only a pile of change and gum wrappers were visible.

"Or Luke? He liked you for some reason."

"Nope. I haven't seen Jessica either." I waited for his silence to end and studied my view. A Canadian quarter sitting about four inches into the water caught my eye. *What's the international exchange rate on wishes?*

"She's probably leaving for the airport," he answered after pausing to clear his throat. "Look for them so they think I'm still there."

"Sure." The throb in my head turned into a pound, matching the pulse on my stuck hand. *When I get out of this well I'll track down the parents of the girl you're having an affair with to keep up your secret.* Keeping

57

secrets was stimulating. Or the rush of blood to my head and rising pulse meant I was about to throw up.

"Thank you for your help today Margaret." Then "click." And he was gone again. I tucked the phone back in and heard another familiar voice.

"Mini," Colin's voice was calm and slow. "Didn't I ask you to stay on the bench?"

"I know but—"

Colin's sigh was deep enough to hear with my head pounding down in a cave. "Don't even start," he said. "Someone needed you right? I needed you too. To stay out of trouble."

"I'm sorry Colin. Can I come out now? My ring is stuck in the grate."

His hands were warm at my waist.

"I'll lift you up a bit to take the weight off, then see if you can wriggle free."

Suspended in the air, my hips held by Colin, I pulled my hand free as my ring loosened and dropped onto the pile of coins. *Clink.*

I hoped that other wishes were luckier than my wedding vows.

He pulled me up and I slid down his body until my feet touched the ground. I turned and came face to face with his grimace. "You are trouble waiting to happen."

"No," I squeaked and stood with a wobble. "Usually I don't leave the house."

He stared into the bottom of the well and shook his head. "After the park closes, I'll have maintenance pull your ring out."

He locked his hand around my elbow and guided me to the Castle entrance. Considering my track record in the last few hours, I was surprised he didn't use hand cuffs. I was one loose buckle away from a full straight jacket.

Chapter 8

Any doctor would diagnose my woozy stomach flutters and light-headedness as the after-effects of hanging upside down for several minutes. But I knew the truth. I was about to cross the drawbridge into Fantasyland. And though the doorway was fixed in place to welcome everyone; in my heart it had opened just for me.

Colin stayed on my right to block the blue-red goose egg hump on my forehead. The camera crew on my left were my own hear no evil, speak no evil, see no evil entourage.

A cameraman walked backward in front of me, making me nervous while he filmed. I imagined myself with that job. I'd take more pictures of sky than anything else. A young woman carrying a large clipboard walked forward guiding him while a third female crew member wearing headphones doubling the size of her skull suspended a microphone from the end of a long pole over my head, fishing for words.

"Walt Disney created Disneyland for parents and children to play together," Colin spoke to the camera. "The park is meant for everyone."

Colin turned to me and placed a large hand on my shoulder. Viewers might think he meant to convey a sign of friendliness, but I knew he was trying to make sure I was still upright.

I must have been dreaming. It was too ridiculous for reality. I would wake up at home with my dream for a family intact. Pretense was comforting.

I waved the international wrist-turning signal all queens automatically know at the small children and parents who were trying to figure out what kind of Southern California celebrity I must be to have my own camera crew.

In my chosen fantasy, I would soak up all the prize had to offer, eat some of the chocolate fudge I eyed in the candy store window and check out the Castle suite. Then I'd go back to bed and wake up in an unsatisfying, yet stable marriage.

Colin led me into the candy store where he spoke into the camera about the importance of my prize while I sampled peanut brittle and let him do all the talking. Since my teeth were stuck together, that worked out well. We left before I had a chance to try the fresh fudge. I'd be back.

I would recognize the back of the most pear-shaped man I'd ever seen even if he wasn't wearing a Chris' Toy Company t-shirt with "The Prez" stenciled on the back.

Crap! I slid behind Colin and buried my face in his jacket.

"Mini? The camera is this way," Colin's voice again had that 'what kind of lunatic am I dealing with' quality. Hiding myself from Chris, I scooted to Colin's other side so the camera crew had to readjust to see me.

"Bee," I stammered and swatted at the clear air. How could I look at Chris without breaking down? It was his daughter with my husband.

Colin signaled the crew to roll again and I inched back behind him.

"Mini. Disneyland is at your feet. Play away." Colin spoke to the camera, his smile not reaching his eyes. He waved me toward the rides, but I held back. "No really, you can let go."

I peeked around his shoulder as Chris boarded the small wood-carved Pinocchio cars and disappeared into the ride.

"Which ride first?" Colin asked, then whispered, "Do you need to lie down?"

"Peter Pan." I stood in the open pretending I hadn't been having an imaginary insect attack. "I'm always a fan of right to left exploration." Plus Chris was on the left.

"Sleeping Beauty is going to Peter Pan. Ready a ship," Colin radioed. The camera crew moved in through the exit and Colin held me back by the arm. He looked straight into my eyes and pointed his finger to my face. "Would it do any good to ask you to mind? Stay. Please." Then he followed the crew.

I was alone for about seven seconds before I heard Luke's voice.

"What's with the cameras?" The kid stood next to me, untwisting a piece of taffy and then popping it into his mouth.

Before I decided which words would help me keep my secret another voice boomed, "There you are, Luke." Great, a family reunion at the exit door. I turned and gave Chris a smile, but my mouth twitched into a lopsided smear. My parents would have known I was guilty of something. "Oh, Margaret," Chris said. "I didn't see you."

That was a damn quick ride. "Hi Chris."

"Where's Michael?" Chris scanned the crowd.

I didn't want to lie to such a nice guy, but if I were him, I wouldn't want to know either. "He's in the bathroom." *That may not be a lie. They do have bathrooms in Vegas, too.*

"We've finished Fantasyland. We're going off to Adventureland. Want to come with us?"

What was I supposed to say? "Don't wait for us. Michael may be in there for a while. Too many corn dogs I'm afraid." *Okay, that is a lie.*

"What a shame," Chris added. "We're off to The Jungle Cruise ride Luke. Want to come?"

"It would be like having cotton candy rubbed into my eyes. So I think no," Luke said. "Margaret was telling me about the camera crew."

"Cameras?" I shrugged, thankful the crew was already loading into Peter Pan and Chris hadn't caught on. "I don't want to keep you Chris."

I made a small wave and moved off when Luke spoke again.

"I think I'll stay with Margaret and Michael for a while," Luke said. "You might be right about these baby rides after all."

"You don't mind Margaret?" Emily squeezed my arm. "You know teenagers never want to hang with their own parents."

"Okay," I croaked as my fantasy melted at my feet.

Chapter 9

Hand in hand, Emily and Chris proved there was no age limit on skipping and left me with their son. I struggled to figure out what to say. And how to get my last few park hours back.

"So...the cameras?" Luke asked. "And what's with the cool badge?"

Too late, my hands flew to cover the badge. "I-uh-won a prize."

"What?"

"Oh," *the best lies are based on the truth,* "a chance to be filmed at Disneyland."

Colin came back to join me. "We're ready for you. Who's this?"

"This is Luke." I pleaded with my eyes for Colin to keep his mouth shut. But I'd never learned to tap SOS in Morse Code. "He's Michael's, my husband's, boss' son."

"The ride will wait for you," Colin said. "Just walk into the exit."

"No waiting in line?" Luke asked. He paid too much attention to adults for a teenager.

"She did win the Key to the Castle."

"What's that?"Luke asked.

"No big deal," I squealed and moved toward the ride. "I get a few rides without lines and the camera crew films me."

"Aren't you going to wait for Michael?" Luke asked.

"Uh, he's still in the bathroom. We might as well go without him."

"Your husband's here?" Colin asked. "I thought you said he'd left for Vegas."

Can I catch a break here? "Uh, no," I said. "He's not leaving for a few hours. Luke's twenty-two-year-old sister is going on the same trip. He didn't want to miss the company fun in Disneyland before he went."

"After you've finished with Fantasyland we'll meet back with Felicity and show you the Castle," Colin added. "She's sent your night things to your room."

"You're sleeping in the Castle?" Luke looked impressed. No small feat for a teenager. "That's your prize?"

I looked past his shoulder at the carousel. "Just a quick night, some rides without lines and the filming. Please don't mention it to anyone. It's no big deal. And I'm kind of shy. Let's go."

The gate was held open for me and we moved through the exit and boarded the flying sailing ships. Suspended from above, we flew over the scenes of Peter and Wendy's trip through Neverland.

Luke was enthralled with the way the lint on his jeans glowed under the black lights, so I was able to relax my tongue that had been tied up into knots. Or as much as I could relax with a cameraman peeking around the edge of his sail, focusing on me. By the time we sailed back into Wendy's window I had a plan. I'd pretend Michael texted me to meet him.

"Mr. Toad's?" Luke asked, before I pulled my phone out of the bag. "Don't tell my dad I like them, but the rides are a lot better without the lines. And thanks, you were right about Innoventions. Those games were great."

"Uh...okay." Michael would want me to entertain his boss' son. What if we went on another ride or two? We waited for the camera crew to board first, then I waved Luke ahead to his own model T car to cut down on conversation and because I wanted to steer. Holding the spinning wheel enhances the adventure through the hollows and adventures of the literary animals. Alone, I spun past the bright scenes on the swerving track. I lived an emotional pinball game. I should have the scenery to match.

My car spun around and Luke and I caught each other laughing. With a nod, we promised not to give away the others' secret of fun.

Temporary comrades, we shared our favorite memories of the park and absorbed Fantasyland—me and Luke and Colin and the film crew.

"Excuse us," Colin barked and parted the crowd between Mr. Toad's and the Pinocchio ride. "Grand Prize winner coming through."

Anyplace else on Earth, a woman being followed by a camera would draw more attention than an occasional point. But in Southern California, the only thing people noticed was that I didn't have to wait in line and they did.

"There's Jiminy," Luke pointed to the first cricket on the Pinocchio ride. "When I was little this ride always scared me, so Mom would keep my eyes away from the scary parts by having me look for the next Jiminy." I tried to focus on the ride and not be pulled back into my mom.

"This is always my favorite part," I pointed to the holographic image of the Blue Fairy as it came into view and dusted Pinocchio with her magic wand before vanishing into twinkles.

The adrenaline created by running from ride to ride carried us through most of Fantasyland. I attempted to ignore Colin while he followed us through each adventure. But the sight of him folded up in the Snow White car was hard to miss. I wanted Colin to leave me alone. Go back to work. But I know he didn't trust me alone again. He'd told me.

I bought Luke an ice cream and a popcorn for myself while I sat and took a moment to stop spinning from back-to-back mounts; first on a golden horse, followed by a small gray elephant. It was easy to be with Luke. He didn't ask any more questions.

"I love this place," I leaned back on the bench of the caged train car. "And no matter how many times I come here, I have to go on these little rides."

"This one's pretty lame," his long legs didn't quite fit into the space; his knees were up to his armpits. Colin and the camera crew were in the car ahead. The microphone stuck out of the cage sides like a giraffe. Colin squeezed in like a gorilla.

I wanted Luke to share and understand what I loved about the park. I'm sure he wanted me to stop talking.

"Oh but look at all the little houses and tiny trees. All that work to create an imaginary world," I said.

"Yeah, right."

"Well, if I had one thing to complain about," I whispered, "it would be the Snow White ride." I covered my mouth with my hand hoping the microphone couldn't pick up my voice.

"Why?"

"It's the ending. You are going along fine, then there's the huge dark battle scene with the dwarves climbing up to the Evil Queen above. You believe the queen is going to win," I said. "Then you turn the corner and Snow and the Prince are living happily ever after. What happened to the queen? Did she win or did the dwarves? I mean I know that the dwarves won from the movie. But the ride leaves it up to interpretation."

"Wow," Luke bobbed his head and his hair bounced over his eyes. "You're crazy about this Disney thing."

"Uh, yeah. Hey look, there's Cinderella's Castle." I pointed up to the miniature replica. He had no idea my level of crazy. A small orange pumpkin sat abandoned on the road down from the castle. If I convinced Felicity to turn a vegetable into a getaway car and I got a job cleaning castles, I might be able to make a life in some kingdom.

I shouldn't indulge in another nauseating spin, but I was entranced. I needed to sit in one of the large tea cups. The pink one.

"Shouldn't we wait for Michael?" Luke asked.

"Who?"

Luke raised his eyebrows.

"Oh, Michael! Yes. Too much spinning." I had forgotten about him for a few minutes. I laughed in a way that I thought would sound casual, but sputtered like I was running out of gas.

"Do you want to call him?"

"Yes. Yes, I was thinking I would do that." I pulled out my phone and pretended to speed dial. "Hey Michael. How are you?"

I bobbed my head for a few seconds—"Uh-huh . . . uh-huh...oh my...oh that's just terrible . . . uh-huh...uh-huh...okay, then ... okay, buh-bye"—and then hung up.

"Okay Luke. Michael's going to one of the Main Street stores for some Pepto Bismo. He's got the...you know," I dropped my voice down to a whisper, "the runs. He wants me to have fun without him. He's that type of guy. Always thinking of my feelings."

Halfway through my lie Luke looked to my right. I was sure he wasn't listening to a thing I'd made up about my caring husband. I followed his look. Two girls were smiling at him.

"Hey," Luke croaked and watched them walked over.

The tallest brunette spoke first. "I didn't know you would be here today."

"My dad's having a company party," Luke's face was pinched and he bounced from one foot to the other while trying to look cool. Puppy love was not a good look.

"Want to go on the ride with us?" the girl asked, pointing to the end of the long winding line.

"Sure," Luke said. I squeezed my hands to keep from clapping. I could leave. "But we should hang with Mrs. Gunderson. She won a prize that gets her to the front of all the lines."

"That is so cool," the short blonde said.

"Do you mind?" Luke asked.

His eyes pleaded with me. *Crap.* He needed a wingman. "Not at all." My face was the pinched one now.

We slid into the tea cup and before I could beg them not to spin, three sets of teenaged hands grabbed the center wheel and we turned into a blur of faces. My mouth hung open by the centrifugal force and I clung to the seat.

"That was great," Luke said as I stumbled off. "We should take on Space Mountain!"

"Uh," I stuttered and the popcorn threatened to reemerge at the thought of another spin. "This is enough for me. You go on without me."

"Thanks for the fastest pass," Luke was holding the girl's hand and in no mood to try to talk me into staying with them. "Too bad about Michael."

"Yeah," I sighed. *Too bad on so many levels not appropriate for expressing to you.* "I'll go meet him." My job was done. I'd been seen by Chris and covered for Michael. I'd entertained Luke and then got him hooked up with a hottie. My fairy godmother powers only worked for so long. Time to go.

"We'll look for you later," Luke walked off, leaving me alone.

With my camera crew. And Colin.

"How long do you need to set up the lighting in the Castle?" Colin asked the girl with the clipboard while he consulted his black and white Classic Mickey watch.

"About twenty minutes," she said.

"Go on ahead and we'll meet you." Colin turned to me and nodded permission. "You have time for one more ride."

A few feet away from Alice in Wonderland, I pointed to the exit and wandered over. I'd finally have a few moments to myself. I climbed into the blue

71

caterpillar car. Before the metal bar was lowered over my lap, Colin slipped beside me.

"For real?" The car moved into the fluorescent storyline. "You can't trust me alone for one minute?"

"No," Colin folded his arms across his chest. His expression looked eerily similar to the Queen of Hearts as she ordered "Off with their heads."

"I guess I can't blame you," I leaned back and checked out the scene of the playing cards painting the roses red as we climbed higher into the ride. "It has been my worst day ever."

The door at the top of the ramp opened and the car rolled outside for a view of The Matterhorn and Small World. For a brief moment, stress fell from my body and I enjoyed the view of the people and attractions under the twinkling park lights.

"Mini, what are you doing here today?" Colin's voice brought my anxiety back up. "You say your husband's not here, but you made quite a show earlier on the phone."

"Well, uh, no he's not here, exactly…" I choked.

"Enough of this bull," Colin's voice lowered, his teeth glowing white under the black lights. "Are you taking me for a schmuck? This story, on top of ransacking a store and ruining a parade? Are you out to take down Disneyland single handedly?"

"Never!" We passed the White Rabbit again. "It was for Luke. Look, this morning at the main gate I found out my husband's having an affair with that kid's sister. His boss's daughter. Okay? They snuck off to Vegas and I've been pretending he's still here while I'm also pretending to be Cinderella in the happiest damn place on earth!"

His jaw dropped. His mouth opened to start to say something then it closed again and he made the low, throat clearing sound I'd begun to recognize as his growl.

"The park is closing early," Colin said as the caterpillar came to a stop at the exit. "Felicity is waiting. You'll have a few minutes with her before the crew films. Are you ready?"

"All my life."

Chapter 10

Blue and gold crested banners brushed my shoulders as I wound up the narrow stone staircase behind Felicity to a massive oak double door held in place by hinges the size of my arms. The electronic key pad was the only evidence my imagination had that I wasn't smack in the middle of the medieval period.

"Go ahead Mini," Felicity dipped into a mock curtsey after swiping a pass key. "Your chamber awaits."

The monstrous doors opened with a light touch. I was a little disappointed not to hear a squeak or groan.

A floor to ceiling window offered a perfect view of Main Street. To my right was a bar area and counter with two barstools. On my left was a side table over which hung a large oil painting of Sleeping Beauty kissed awake by her prince. Between the bar and the window was a seating area and entertainment center next to a round dining table with a bowl of white roses that changed from pink to blue with a flick from a rotating light in the ceiling. Their velvety touch and fragrant aroma proved they were real.

A gossamer-draped canopy bed, so high it had a ladder, dominated the room. I stepped up to the top and flopped face down on the royal blue satin coverlet and sunk into the deep goose down. *This is officially the nicest room I'd ever been in.* Maybe I wouldn't go home tonight.

We never had a honeymoon. My new in-law's call caught us at the airport before we boarded the plane for Hawaii.

"There's been an accident," Michael had said. Those were the last words I remembered for quite some time.

Somewhere during those lost months Michael had pulled me out of nursing school two semesters before graduation. It would have been too hard for me to be around sick and hurt people after my parents died, he'd said.

One morning, a year after their death, I had emerged from my fog.

Michael had suggested that I go into teaching a foreign language with all the French I'd already studied, though he thought I should switch to Spanish to increase my odds at getting a good job. After all we did live in California, where Spanish was the second language. It made sense. It also meant starting over. So I returned to college.

Michael had doted over me. He always insisted I drove straight home from school and rest. He said he didn't want me to sink back into the darkness of loss. I trusted him. I wasn't able to trust myself. I needed someone like him to take care of me, to call the shots.

A few units shy of my BA in Spanish, Michael thought I should sign up for the double major in French to brush up and then take the teaching credential course. Another two-and-a- half years of school.

It had sounded like a good plan. I wasn't in a hurry.

I ached for mom and dad, but there was another hole growing inside me. I wanted a baby. A blood link.

Felicity pulled back the floor-to-ceiling drapes in the corner of the bedroom revealing a large glass balcony door labeled "Open Only During Non-Park Hours."

"I love this Castle, but my favorite fairy tale was always Snow White," Felicity said. "I liked scary stories when I was little and loved being frightened by the witch."

I wandered into the bathroom large enough for four extroverts to use at one time. The whirlpool tub took center stage with a marbled, clear glass shower stall. A long double sink beside the tub held every possible necessity from Q-tips to a bowl of wrapped chocolates. At the far end was a dressing area and walk-in closet.

My cell phone rang. I didn't need caller ID to know it was Michael. I moved into the water closet and closed the door so Felicity wouldn't witness my panic. I tested to see if I could keep his secret.

"Hello," I squeaked when the cool porcelain of the bidet touched my leg.

"What's up Margaret?" Michael's voice sounded tired. I didn't want to think of what had worn him out. "You squeak when you are nervous. Is everything clear?"

"I think I should probably go back and finish school. Either nursing or teaching. Which do you think I should pick?" I babbled without taking a breath—testing the waters to see if I could convince him to back me through school one more time. "It can't be too interesting for you to have a college dropout for a wife. I could help you more if I have something interesting to talk about…"

"Margaret," Michael sighed, his voice low. "You don't need to stress yourself out on this. You do a great job on the putting green. That's useful. Did you see Chris?"

"You're safe. Your boss doesn't suspect." I wasn't sure if he'd be excited or annoyed that I'd spent so much time with Luke. No sense risking it. Another lie by omission.

"That's good." He laughed. He wasn't worried about his affair. He had no idea what I'd seen. I wanted to hurl one thousand questions and accusations, but I didn't want to hear any of the answers.

During the pause where I would have bet he waited for me to ask him about his day, I listened to his slow breathing, the tinkling of slot machines and what might have been the sound of Jessica waiting for him to finish talking to his wife so they could continue their affair.

"You won't be able to reach me on my cell tomorrow, so don't try to call me," he said. "I'll call you when I have a break. Love you." He clicked off.

I stared at the phone trying to make sense of what happened to my world.

Felicity knocked. "Are you okay dear?"

Determined to look like a normal person, I opened the door with a smile plastered on my face. When Felicity touched my arm in a show of support I melted and had to fight the urge to throw myself bawling into her arms. "It's my husband. He left the park early today to watch an air show in Vegas. He didn't want his boss to know."

"It's understandable to miss him. It's always more fun to share Disneyland with someone you love."

"He wouldn't want to share it. Not with me. He doesn't love Disneyland the way I do," I sighed, then sagged onto the beautiful bed in pure melodramatic fashion. "Or me the way he used to. I'm not sure how he feels now."

"I'm sure you're wrong. You're a lovely person."

I wanted all lying to stop. Except to Michael. "If I were, then Michael wouldn't have been kissing the boss' daughter at the gate on their way out this morning for two nights in Las Vegas."

"Oh Dear."

"Yep." I wasn't ready for her sympathy. I didn't want the tears that had been threatening to start falling again. They might never stop.

Felicity's mouth twisted for a moment and she formulated her words. "It's none of my business, but does he know you saw him?"

"No," I said into the comforter. "He doesn't know about this prize either. I figure I'll keep my secret and he'll keep his. Of course I won't be able to stay. I'll have to leave tonight to get home and figure out a way to deal with this." The mountain of pillows that topped the canopied bed enveloped me in softness.

"So you're going to pretend you didn't see anything?" Felicity sat on the bed next to me. I hoisted myself up into a sitting position.

"My first thought was to pack up and leave before he gets back, which is still an option," I rubbed my eyes, pressing tears back in. "But he's the only family I have. There's no one else left. Plus I have no skills or job options. I went to college for years and never graduated with any degree. I'm not a closer."

"You could go back to school," she offered. "Finish whichever area you are the most happiest with. You never know until you try. You need to believe in yourself."

"Who'd want a teacher, nurse, entertainer and gardener who never finished anything in her life?" She wiped my tears off with a warm touch.

"I understand Mini. I'll tell the camera crew to stand down." She got up and walked to the balcony door. "At least check out the view before you go. I'll leave your card active and your room ready in case you change your mind. Goodbye dear. It was a pleasure."

An hour later, I washed my face and hands, then used one of the lotions left on the counter, their lids black with mouse ears on top. The face in the mirror looked different. The shock had worn off. *Let the bleeding begin.*

I'd screwed up several times today butting in to help people and causing problems. I needed to go home and practice my "I didn't see you cheating" face. I'd have to pretend. I had no choice. At least until I thought of a way out.

I picked up a feathered writing pen from the desk, dropped the souvenir in my purse and stepped out on the balcony for one look before I left.

The sparkling twinkle strands had been replaced by large can lights that brightened the closed park to near daylight. Crews rolled by with watering trucks, street cleaners and supply bins like a busy morning on a city street.

A worker drew up a cart and knelt in the bed of pansies and began pulling out each pink bundle. I watched him work from the back—his blond hair, his muscles rippling under his tight t-shirt. Mesmerized by the rhythm of his work, I jumped when he turned to face me.

I ducked under the railing and crawled back into the room with all the dignity I could muster from my knees.

Dragging my regrets down the stone staircase like a long velvet train, I said goodbye to the best thing that had ever happened to me and crossed the drawbridge back to the second worse thing ever – my screwed up marriage.

I circled a sign post pointing to the different lands. Even with the Key to the Castle I hadn't seen half of the park. I wandered off the exit track toward one of the spots Ariel waits for photographs. Although the park was closed, scores of cleaners scurried around, watering, sweeping, emptying trash containers. I slipped past the velvet rope and sat at the water's edge.

In the distance, I heard the sound of someone singing. A deep male voice sang along with the Disney tunes piped over the park. In my dark, secluded spot next to the bubbling water I closed my eyes and sung along with one of my favorites—'A Dream is a Wish Your Heart Makes.'

Some of the heaviness I'd carried on my chest all day lifted as I sang. 'Kiss the Girl' started next and I channeled Ariel by trailing my fingertips in the water. Strong work lights created the reflection of the trees on the water's surface. I had no idea how to pretend to save my old life. Whatever happened, I would have to figure this out alone.

"Hello," a voice boomed. I jumped up and slipped down the rock and up to my armpits in the cold water.

"Ah!" I turned toward the deep, just rolled-out-of-bed voice of a man.

"Out for a walk Margaret?" Even wearing a gardener's uniform smelling of fertilizer and dirt, I'd recognize that smiling face anywhere. A sparkle of light may even have bounced off his white teeth. Or maybe I was having a stroke.

"My Prince?"

Chapter 11

Graceful as possible I ignored his outstretched hand and climbed back to dry land. I'd nearly completed my slippery extrication with some poise until air escaped my wet shoes like my feet had gas.

"Are you all right Margaret?" he smiled and glanced down my drenched front to the puddle at my feet. I followed his stare to see that beige may be serviceable, but only practical when soaked if I were trying to win a wet t-shirt contest.

"Fine," I squeaked, pulling the shirt away from my body with a loud suction. "How did you know my name?"

"I remember you from the parade." He grabbed my elbow to keep me upright when my shoes slipped on the concrete. "You're the grand prize winner."

"Call me Mini."

"I'm Peter. I play Prince Charming."

"I know. I remember." The warmth of his hand spread up my arm. "You saved me."

"That was easy. What you did," he stopped at a gardener's cart and focused straight into my eyes, "was courageous. Jumping in front of that float to save that little boy."

"He didn't need me," I blushed.

83

"That doesn't take away from your bravery. I find courage sexy in a woman."

Oh, God. My free hand pulled the wet fabric away from magnifying exactly how cold wet could be in the cool night air. "I'm married," I blurted.

"Of course you are," he smiled. "So where is he?"

"Uh..." *At home baking cookies, out polishing his gun collection, in the bathroom....* "He's in Vegas with his girlfriend."

The truth, no matter how bad was so much easier than lying.

"So you're leaving him."

My chest constricted when I tried to remember to breathe. *Was I having this intimate conversation with a gorgeous hunk that couldn't keep his eyes off my soggy breasts? Was it another part of today's fantasy?*

"It's an early mid-life crisis," I rationalized. "He's coming back to me now that it will be out of his system."

"Pansy?"

"Excuse me?"

He released my hand and placed a purple flower ball on my palm. "Want to help me plant? I have this entire section to redo before the park reopens in the morning."

"I don't know." How could I plant pansies with a stranger?

"We could sing a few more songs. You're pretty good," he said.

I shook my head trying to figure out if I was awake, asleep or insane. "In college maybe. I'm pretty rusty."

He bent down near my feet and used a small trowel to open up a hole, then raised his hand up to mine. I passed the flower.

84

"Where did you go to school?" he patted the plant into its new bed, then made another hole.

I reached over to the cart and loosened another plant from the plastic container, trying to ignore the trickle of cold water running down my leg. "UCLA. And you?" I squeaked. The lecherous part of me that I'd just realized existed, prayed he didn't say high school. Was this how Michael's libido erupted when he'd met Jessica?

"The same! I finished my masters and work here while I audition."

"You didn't know Mrs. Garcia?"

"She was my faculty advisor. And a great teacher."

"I agree. It's been a long time, but I miss her, although she always gave me a hard time for favoring Charlie Daniel's songs."

"She would have. For her it's Broadway all the way," he finished the row, then adjusted his kneel to begin another. I watched the muscles in his back ripple. "You must have been pretty good to be in her classes."

"I was okay." I wiggled against my wet, bunched-up underwear as I bent to reach the plants. "But my husband thought I'd be a great nurse, so I switched majors. It's pretty hard to make a living in the theatre."

"I will," he said. "You have to believe in yourself."

"I've heard that."

He stood up and turned to face me, brushing off his hands. "You're cold."

"Uh!" I looked down at my personal thermostats, wrapped my arms over my chest and dashed away. "I gotta go."

"I'll see you tomorrow," he called.

I ran back to the Castle room and hid next to the window like a fifteen-year-old who'd been caught staring at her crush. An envelope marked 'Maintenance' in large letters, left at my bedside slammed me back to the other end of my youth. I'd almost left without the ring.

Chapter 12

The package opened in one quick pull and the ring flipped out onto the bed. The tasteful, third-carat diamond solitaire in a white gold setting; not too big, not too small, had been selected by Michael hours before he'd asked me to marry him.

On Michael's graduation day he had left the ceremony with me and his parents for a dinner at his favorite restaurant. After the salad course, he'd stood up and proposed in front of his parents.

"My internship with Chris' Toy Company has turned into a real job. Now only being married to this woman will complete my life." He'd slapped the ring on before I ever had a chance to answer. I never did accept. I would have though, given the chance.

The plain wedding band had been soldered on sometime during that first year of darkness.

It still looked the same—color, shape, even after being caught in a grate. Even after discovering I wasn't Michael's true love. I slipped it into the coin section of my organizer wallet. I couldn't put it on. Yet.

Every choice I'd made since witnessing the hideous kiss had ended with me falling on my face. I couldn't rush the most important decision of my life.

I peeled my wet clothes off, hung them on the shower door and hit them with the hair dryer after I'd snuggled into the fluffy terry robe. I managed to make them warm and wet. I'd have to wait a while before going home.

Home. My childhood home and now Michael's house. I've tried hard to make it so. Ever since the reading of the will.

The first time I had seen Michael angry was the day it was read.

"I don't want to go," I had cried.

"How would it look if their only child didn't show up for the reading of the will? They can't give me any information unless you're present," Michael had said. "It's what your parents would have wanted."

That had done it. I'd climbed off the rumpled bed and put on clothes for the first time since their funeral two days before. The same black dress. My tear–soaked face was puffy beyond recognition. It was too painful to look at myself. I could never see them again. Never prove to them that Michael was right for me.

I don't recall how we got to the lawyer's office but I do remember the moment Michael heard about the house.

"All their assets are being held in a trust for Margaret," the lawyer had said. "A small dividend may be allocated each year and the estate in Anaheim Hills may be occupied. But the full amount of the inheritance may not be accessed, nor the house sold, while Margaret is married to Michael Gunderson."

"Son of a bitch," Michael had yelled. "He had it in for me."

"He liked you," I stumbled.

"How could he do this to me?"

"Die?" I'd squeezed the tattered bits of tissue in my hand.

"Cut me out like this."

I had rubbed his shoulders and used a soothing voice, desperate to make him feel better. "I'm sure he was just upset. He would have changed his mind once he got to know you."

"You live in a fantasyland if you believe that."

Michael started packing for the move when we stepped into our apartment door.

"I thought you wouldn't want to live there," I had said.

"Are you kidding? That's what he would want me to feel. But I'll live in his house and make it mine."

We went to the house and I had returned to the comfort of my room, took a sleeping pill at Michael's insistence and slept. I woke the next day to the sound of movers. Michael had hired a crew to empty my parent's bedroom.

"What are you doing?" I had screeched when their mattresses were being wedged out into the hallway.

"You can't expect me to stay in your room? I don't want to be a kid forever. This is the master bedroom."

Family photos that covered my parent's dresser were being loaded into cardboard boxes. "But what are you going to do with everything?"

"Goodwill. There's a truck outside."

"But Michael. These are my parents' things, I need time to figure out what to do. I need time to adjust."

He had pulled me into his arms. "I know honey. It was terrible, what your Dad did, putting you between them and your husband. Cleaning these things out will help you heal. Besides I know you wouldn't want to hurt me."

Stuck between wanting something to remember them by and not hurting Michael's feelings, I'd scrambled for words to stop him. "Some of these antiques are valuable," I'd said. Maybe we should leave them in the attic and see later if there's any worth."

"Good thinking. We could use the cash."

In the end, I was able to have the terms of the will adjusted. We spent most of the immediate money on lawyers and the house went into community property. It still couldn't be sold while we were married, but when it was sold, he'd get half.

Dad wanted to give me the house. I could leave Michael any time I wanted. But I'd have no car, no cash, no job, no family, no friends and no place to live until my parent's legacy was disposed.

"Face it Min," I told my reflection in the bathroom mirror and tried the hairdryer again on my blouse. "You screwed yourself on this one."

If he wanted to keep me as his wife, I would play along. At least long enough to think of another way out.

I snuggled on the bed while I waited for my clothes to dry and formulated a small plan to spend time in my attic before Michael returned, to see if anything was left of my childhood.

My eyes stung as I laid my head back against the pile of pillows and a line of tears rolled into my ear. I couldn't even cry right.

Chapter 13

"Tap, Tap, Tap."

"Hmm," I stretched out long against the soft sheets ignoring the sound while trying to return to my dream... I was about to be kissed by a handsome prince.

"Knock, knock." The growing sound forced my eyes open. My pupils adjusted to the soft light filtering through the blue gossamer bed curtains while my mind caught up with the reality that I was still in the Castle. *I have to get out of here. I have so much to do before he returns from adultery.*

I fought my way through the down blanket and pile of lace pillows to find myself naked. I slipped into the robe and pulled open the door. Felicity's raised hand almost knocked on my face.

"Good morning dear," she smiled. "I'm so glad you decided to stay."

"But I..."

"Where shall I put the food?" asked a white-coated waiter behind her who pushed a multi-layer tray.

"Right over here," Felicity waved toward the small dining table and pulled up a second chair. "I thought you might enjoy some company for breakfast and I'm starving."

"Uh, sure." The smell of food filled the room. "Since you went to all this trouble. But I'm still leaving. I fell asleep by mistake."

"Well at least have something to eat," Felicity smoothed down the hair on the top of my head that must have been sticking straight up, then patted the chair next to her.

The waiter moved the vase of roses and covered the tabletop with piles of pancakes, sausages, rolls and fruit.

"I wasn't sure what you like besides popcorn and corndogs," Felicity said. "So I brought a little of everything."

"I usually eat a bowl of cereal. Michael loves Cream of Wheat."

"Try a little of everything."

I selected a small Mickey-shaped pancake.

Felicity pulled a triangle of powdered-sugar dusted French toast and doused it with syrup, then handed me the jar.

I poured the syrup over Mickey's face, then cut off one ear and popped it into my mouth. I heard the angels sing as the fluffy white pancake melted into maple goodness on my tongue and the heavenly carbs landed on my breasts—the only part of me that gained weight.

"You had quite a day yesterday Mini," Felicity said, taking a dainty bite out of an enormous cinnamon roll.

"Don't remind me," I sputtered, taking a roll in my ringless left hand, my right held the next bite of pancake. The cinnamon layers crunched in my mouth while a drip of icing rolled warm down my chin. "Colin must hate me."

"He doesn't open up about his emotions," she laughed. "But I'm sure he doesn't hate you."

"I couldn't tell if he thought I was crazy or out to bring down Disneyland. I can't blame him I guess. I couldn't do anything but get into trouble yesterday." *Is that reason number seventeen or eighteen why I have to go back to my pretend marriage?*

"That's not how I remember it," Felicity spooned an egg sausage mixture that smelled of apples and sweet onions onto her plate and offered me the spoon.

I scooped some onto my plate.

"From the parade footage of our security camera," Felicity added, "I saw a caring individual who risked her own safety to help a small child. If that boy hadn't been wearing a harness, it could have been serious."

"He didn't need my help." I polished off the pancake and started working on the eggs, using the rest of the cinnamon roll as a scooper.

"But you didn't know that. You reacted on instinct and that was good." She passed the fruit tray and I took a bite of kiwi and strawberry. "Have you worked with children before?"

"Not unless you count babysitting when I was fifteen."

"Then I'd believe you had good parents. People learn the best when they have great role models."

"They were great," I grabbed a chocolate-glazed donut and admired the thick white line encircling it. A summer job at a bakery had taught me the wider the white line, the lighter the donut. "But I don't think I learned much from them. They were kind and fun. Everyone loved them."

93

They deserved much better from me. I should have listened to them when they tried to steer me away from Michael. Stuffed, I put down my fork and the last half of the sweet.

"I'm sorry," Felicity squeezed my hand. "Does talking about your parents make you sad?"

"No. I think about them all the time, but I don't talk about them much." I topped off the coffee in our cups and sat back, eager to take the focus off me before I cried again. "Tell me about your kids."

"They're all married," Felicity took the hint. "And I have seven grandchildren. One is already in college. I can't believe how fast time has gone. It seems like last week when I first came to the park. Opening day 1955."

"You're kidding!" I leaned forward on the table, covering my elbow in syrup. Felicity had reached rock star status in my book.

"I was ten and knew immediately I never wanted to leave," she said.

"What was it like?"

"Hot!" Felicity laughed. "And crowded. The lines for everything went on forever. But the magic was already here. When I heard Walt welcome us into Fantasyland, it was like he spoke straight to me."

"I know what you mean!" I eyed the rest of the food plates and wondered what else I could fit in. "No matter how crowded the park is; it's still a personal experience." I decided I had room for one more pancake since I was already wearing the syrup.

"As soon as I was old enough, I started working summers and school vacations," she added. "I've worked in every land, but it was Guest Services that I loved. Every day I get to walk through the park with a newcomer and see the park through fresh eyes."

"Wow!" I talked over the fluffiness packed into my cheeks. "I couldn't think of a more perfect tour guide than you. You make people so welcome—anything's possible. You are a fairy godmother."

Felicity laughed and raised her arm pretending to hold a wand. "Bibbidi-bobbidi-boo!" she sang out.

I imagined sparkles of light flowing from her fingertips when she waved her hand through the air like a Hawaiian dancer. "So if I could make any wish come true," she asked, "what do you want to do today?"

Figure out how to earn enough to support myself and buy half of my house. "Well, I always mow the front lawn on Mondays."

"That sounds like a have-to," she smiled. "What do you *want* to do? What would make you happy?"

"I don't know. I haven't thought of that in a long time."

I could fly to Vegas and demand Michael stop seeing Jessica and then go into marriage counseling.

But I didn't want to face him. I wanted to stay at the park for the day, have fun and forget for a while that my marriage was over and I'd be alone. But I had to go.

"I'm sure you know in your heart what's best." Felicity stood up and held out her hand when I couldn't find words to answer her question. "Take a little time to walk around the park before you go. It always helps me clear my head."

I took her hand and didn't want to let go. "Thanks for everything."

"You're welcome dear," she patted my shoulder. "And we'll talk again. My number is in the prize packet. Call me when you decide what to do with your winnings."

"I forgot that there's more," I waved at the glorious room, scented in breakfast meats.

"Think about it. You do have some things going for you. You have won the largest prize in Disneyland's history."

Chapter 14

The wrinkles I tried to smooth in the clothes I'd left to dry overnight on the shower door bounced right back like yesterday's problems.

At least at this point I had a plan. A lousy plan—but a direction. I would go through the attic for any treasures I could protect before he got back, do my chores and say nothing when Michael returns. There was still a possibility one day I could forget about it, if it was a one-time thing. If I couldn't, going home would give me time to think my way out of my marriage. He'd never know that I'd seen him. Not until I was sure of my next move.

The lanyard I'd draped over my neck with unlimited Disney power gave me courage. I had won. At something. I couldn't take on all that the prize had to offer without Michael finding out and spoiling it. But I could sneak to the park anytime I wanted while he was at work or on one of his sports trips. I tried not to think of Jessica as a triathlon.

Timed by the Sleeping Beauty clock, exactly five minutes of pity was all I allowed before I pulled open the door to leave.

A mountain of velvet and glitter blocked my path. The wheels of an overflowing rack just missed my toes, pushed by a thin woman wearing a tape measure necklace and a mouth full of straight pins tipped in red and blue.

"What's this?"

"Your costume for the parade," she said through one corner of her wrinkled mouth. "A queen needs something elegant." She eyed my clothes and didn't flinch at the wrinkles or the dirt marks on my knees caused by falling out of grace so many times yesterday.

"But I'm not going to…"

"Off with your clothes Martha." She waved her hands then began unloading fabrics and notions from her rack.

"It's Mini, and I'm sorry, but I'm leaving," she grabbed my purse with one hand and pulled. "Okay, okay. A few more minutes won't matter."

The single way out was through velvet, so I stripped and she began measuring, then pulled a half-finished skirt over my head. A gold bodice was pinned at my shoulders and she tugged on two puffy gold and blue sleeves.

Satisfied that I was connected she stood back and scrawled in her notebook with a fierceness that dared the pen in her hand not to break. "So much to do," she muttered. "Gotta hurry." Her radio went off and she listened to a static reply.

"I'll be right back," she slipped out the door and I walked to the full-length mirror. I was sorry I wasn't going to get to be the queen in the parade. Even unfinished, the dress was lovely and even made me think I looked beautiful—a feeling I hadn't had since I'd first tried on my wedding gown. I brushed my bangs to the side in an unapproved hairstyle. Michael may not like it, but it was better cover for the goose egg on my forehead that had morphed into a light green/purple bruise.

Ten minutes later she hadn't returned so I twisted and turned, trying to remove the pins so I could escape, but I couldn't reach any of them. I tried to sit down, but winced when a sharp point made contact at my lower back.

I had no idea what to do. I opened the door and stepped out into the hallway. No one.

Another twenty minutes passed and still no sign. She'd forgotten I was here and I needed someone to free me so I called Felicity. No answer. I peeked back out into the empty hall again. The smell of fresh popcorn tugged at my nose. Pacing complete, I grabbed my Disney pass and tiptoed downstairs.

Fear of being stabbed by the pins kept my posture erect and made for a regal descent.

I peeked out at the bottom. Fantasyland was full of strollers and children, but no sign of the dresser or Felicity. It was already a warm morning and the thick velvet had started several drips of sweat that ran down my sides. *A Mickey ice cream makes sense.* I slid into line and no one batted an eye. At Disneyland you could be dressed in a queen's gown and still fit in.

I waited my turn and watched a little girl about four years old swinging on the chain in front of the Peter Pan ride.

I turned back with my frozen bar, looking for a female to unpin me, when I saw the girl slip and flip over the chain. I was running before her head smacked the concrete and kneeled beside her when the first screams made it out of her mouth.

With a tender touch I held the Popsicle against her head while I tried to catch her attention to check if her eyes were dilating.

My rusty nursing skills made me feel professional until the tiara that I'd forgotten was on my head slipped onto my nose. The little girl's ear piercing cries stopped and focused on me.

"Eres una Princessa?" She asked me in Spanish if I were a princess.

"Soy una Reina del helado," I dusted off my Spanish and claimed ice cream royalty. "See" I moved the popsicle to show her the frozen treat, then moved it back to the bump that had sprouted. "Helado es muy bueno."

"Will she be all right?" The mom asked with a thick accent.

"I'm sure she'll be fine. But she'll need to go to first aid." The voice behind me was Colin's.

I decided not to face him, but stared at the girl. "Como te llamas?"

"Tanya," she looked past me to Colin and her mother. "La Reina es bonita."

"Si!" Colin agreed.

"Don't be silly," I blushed at arrival of the first aid crew. "Tu eres bonita."

"You know your way around a cold pack," the female attendant said. "You've had some first aid training?"

"Two years in nursing school."

Tanya frowned at the first aid crew member. "No quiero ir."

"She's afraid of doctors." Her mother whispered.

I told Tanya in Spanish that if she was good and went with the nice people to First Aid, that I would let her wear my tiara.

She nodded yes, her eyes on the crown.

The crew lifted Tanya on a hard board. I straightened up, but stumbled when the skirts tangled in my legs. Colin grabbed me by the waist and lifted me easily to my feet.

He put me down, but his arms stayed at my waist. I was pinned to his jacket like a day-old prom corsage. I leaned back into his arms to release the tension, his chest strong.

"Sorry," I muttered. He unpinned one spot only to be caught by another. "Can we do this some other place less obvious?" The crowd had stopped staring at Tanya and focused on me.

We walked the few yards to the Castle door and tried not to slip. Unable to walk up the stairs to my room together, we huddled at the bottom.

Colin's hand was a straight pin away from first base while I tried to disengage his sleeves.

"Hold still. Let me try," I said.

"It's unreal what happens around you." Colin's voice was soft on my ear, his breath warm on my neck.

"I didn't knock the girl down," I pulled the pin free of his left sleeve and resisted the urge to stick it in his arm. "I wanted some help getting out of the dress."

"That wasn't what I meant," He pulled his right arm free. "I'm glad you were there for her. You're a very easy…"

A cool draft brushed my legs as the skirt slipped to a velvety puddle around my legs.

101

"Ah!" I grabbed at the fabric, stabbing my leg with pins in a desperate attempt to cover my Minnie Mouse panties.

Chapter 15

"Sorry I was gone so long Mini," the dresser spoke through the side of her mouth even though she held no pins. She took the final measurements and unfastened the rest of the pieces. "Ariel's tail was caught in her rotating chair and I wanted to undo her without tearing the fabric."

"I had a costume malfunction of my own." I turned for my clothes that I'd left on the bed but it had been made up and my clothes were gone.

"Where are my things?" I knelt on the side of the bed in my underwear to look underneath.

"They were dirty," the woman said. "I sent them to be cleaned. They'll be back in a couple of hours."

"Hours? What am I supposed to do?" The only way to keep my secret and Michael's was to get home, do the chores and make it look like nothing was amiss. *He can't know my secret. He doesn't deserve to know.*

"Don't worry," Felicity walked into the room. "I had a Disney wardrobe sent over in your size. I'm sure you'll find something you like in the armoire."

"Wardrobe?" I opened the doors at the rainbow of all my favorite colors lime green, hot pink and ocean blue. Michael hated brights. "I couldn't."

"It's all part of the Key to the Castle," she pulled open a full shoe drawer. "I guessed at your size. You're a seven, right?"

The dresser rolled out the cart when my phone rang. I collapsed onto the bed. This was it. He was going to tell me he was not coming back. If we broke up for good, I wanted to be the one to tell him.

"Good morning Margaret," his voice was upbeat and rested. Cheating agreed with him. "How was your night without me? Did you sleep okay?"

"Fine." That sounded better than admitting I'd cried myself to sleep.

"I worried you wouldn't have slept a wink. All alone in the house." His sounded soft and caring.

"I slept like a rock." *Right after I went to bed with a prince. Okay, flower bed.*

"Oh? You must have been exhausted from the stress of the day at the park." He had no idea. "This has been quite a tough day so far. I've been on my feet since six a.m. and have a whole day ahead still. Don't forget to finish the lawn patches today. I'm having friends over for putting Wednesday night and it needs to be perfect."

"You're coming home?" That sounded stupid. "I mean you're having a party when you come home?"

"Like every Wednesday night, Margaret, for about a year, and this week is our birthday," Michael's sigh spoke volumes on my calendar integrity. "Nothing has changed."

"Nothing?" Everything had changed for me.

"We must have a bad connection or something," Michael said. "You can't hear me? I'll call back later to check in. Remember I'll be back tomorrow and you won't be alone anymore. Anything you need to tell me?"

A perfect opening to say, *"I saw you with her."* Or I could have started with, *"I won a prize worth more money than you make in years."* But I didn't. "You're right. Nothing's changed. Goodbye Michael." I stared at the phone for several minutes while I tried to figure out what was happening to me. Michael didn't seem to want a divorce. He might want to keep his wife/greens-keeper. How long could I keep his secret? Forever?

"What's next Mini?" Felicity asked.

"I don't know." I said, picking up a pair of blue shorts. *Do I dare wear them? Dare to go out today and start living my secret life?* "I want to see the rest of the park."

I tied the laces on the white sneakers with pink Minnie Mouse shaped eyelets to finish off my outfit that screamed Disney fanatic. In these new shoes I could run faster and jump higher. At least in my imagination. And I was going to let my imagination out to play. I needed it to help me find my way.

"Your purse is heavy," Felicity picked it up for me. "Do you need it all?"

"Habit, I guess," I grabbed the bulky bag that I had hauled all over Fantasyland yesterday and dumped it out on the bed. I left the organizer, Michael's ticket package, what was left of my makeup, and his epinephrine in case he was stung by a bee.

Several pounds lighter, I backtracked through Sleeping Beauty's Castle and reentered the park.

Chapter 16

Visions of the last frozen treat melting against the little girl's head spoiled that particular snack for the time being so I went back to the same vendor and picked up a thick chocolate-crusted vanilla bar shaped in the familiar silhouette.

"Great job helping that little girl Mini!" the young lady said and reached into the deep freezer. "I can't believe how fast you ran. Especially in that dress!"

I wasn't used to compliments, or the fact that strangers knew my name.

"Thanks," I said. "It seemed like slow motion to me, though. I saw her going over and bolted. It would have been a little more graceful not pinned into a costume." *Not to mention, I wouldn't have been showing off my underwear.*

"Everyone was super impressed," she said. "I heard the paramedics say so."

"Well I have had some nursing training. I guess it kicked in." I bit a hunk of the chocolate off one ear and waved goodbye. Maybe nursing could be my escape. Although, it would take two more years in school. If I talked Michael into paying for it, leaving him would be an option—in case having a Jessica was habit forming. I wandered through Fantasyland and behind Thunder Mountain, looking into each of the stores on my way. I walked along the sidewalk of River of America and decided to head to Splash Mountain.

107

I would go on Splash Mountain every time with my parents—in my own way. Dad would tease me through the line every forty five seconds when a log would drop down the thirty-foot water shoot and the screaming would erupt. That didn't bother me at all. Mom and I would gush over the Brer Fox and Brer Rabbit vignettes along the path and sing Zippidy Do Da together. I couldn't be afraid of something I knew I could bail out on at the end of the line.

At the point where the wet logs were rolling up to the entrance Mom and I would wave goodbye to Dad and hit the last exit. We'd wait outside satisfied that I'd seen all the best of the ride without risking my life.

"Come on Mini," Dad would repeat. "Just once and you'll be hooked. You'll love it."

I'd trusted Dad in all things. Except this. He'd talked me into Space Mountain the year before and I'd thrown up for an hour followed by another thirty minutes of quiet weeping. He'd always tried to tell me I must have eaten something bad. That it wouldn't be like that if I gave it another try. I never did.

The salty heat of the popcorn truck called me over for sustenance and the sweet, salty balance I would need during the long line. The teenager filling my large box called me by name too, remembering me from yesterday.

I saw Colin standing with a crew of visitors all wearing suits and ties near the start of the line.

"Hey Mini," Colin excused himself from the crowd. "Going on Splash Mountain next? Need a partner?"

I tried not to make eye contact since the last time I'd seen him I was in my underwear. "I've never gone on the ride—too scared. But I do like to walk through and check everything out. I'm good alone."

My Key to the Castle was a magnet for attention, even without the camera crew. Wanting to slide under the radar, I tucked it into my shirt before walking under a wooden train bridge to the start of the line, behind the split rail fence.

The clay-colored Splash Mountain jutted out into Critter Country, half circled by a line that lasts two to three hundred times the length of the ride. I averted my eyes from the screens placed on the walls which showed riders piled single file into log-shaped cars that climbed through the mountain before plunging down the waterfall of death. I wasn't going down that path, but I didn't need to watch others take the fateful plunge.

A combination of voices all talking at the same time turned out to be a group of three girls in line behind me.

"I hope we don't fall out of the log," the tallest girl teased.

"Oh yes," another said. "I hear they lose single riders most often. Erica, isn't it your turn to ride alone?" A short blond girl between them chewed at her bottom lip and had her arms wrapped around her middle like she was trying to hold her pounding heart in her chest.

Perhaps I have a special insight into the lives of other mortals, that I am a protector of all those weak and mistreated. Or that it takes a chicken to know a chicken. Erica wanted to be anywhere else.

The weekday line moved fast enough for me to enjoy the familiar scenes from the old Brer Rabbit stories, but slow enough to see the panic rising in Erica that made me want to reach the exit even faster than usual. The girls continued to harass her. Erica said "stop it guys," twice, then stopped talking.

Every word about the upcoming plunge pushed my stomach down further until I was stepping on it with each foot closer to the carts. I even stopped eating. They scared the hell out of me and I didn't plan on riding.

"It's so awful," Erica squeaked. "I don't think I can do it."

"Then wait by Winnie the Pooh, with the other babies." The tall girl said again.

"I'll go," she whimpered. More afraid of her friends' teasing than the ride.

The sight of the exit brought its usual relief when I was bumped from behind and the rest of the popcorn spilled on the pseudo rock floor.

"I'm sorry. She pushed me," Erica said.

"That's okay," I smiled, trying to calm her even though I was ready to bolt. "It was an extra large. I need to cut myself off for a while." Her meager smile showed me distraction was the right track.

"You must love popcorn."

"I love everything they sell here. I haven't stopped eating since I arrived yesterday and I still haven't tasted everything. I have my eye on some fudge I saw them making through a window on Main Street for later!"

She giggled. "So do you like this ride?"

"I don't know. I've never done it." Telling the truth was easier no matter how lame I sounded. "I always go through the line to check out the scenes and storyline, then at the end I bail." I waved my hand toward the exits flight attendant style.

"Really?" Her eyes hopeful until her friends laughed.

"It's no big deal Erica," the other girl said. "You should try the drop at Jurassic Park ride at Universal Studios. From the top of this drop you only have time to say 'shit' before you hit the bottom. During the Jurassic fall you have time to say, 'shit, are we still falling?'"

The color that drained from Erica's face said she wasn't comforted by that analogy. The line moved and we were about to be routed into loading sections. I looked at the exit—my safety hatch.

"You can bail out with me if you want to Erica," I offered. "I'll wait with you."

"Yeah go ahead and wait with the old lady," the louder girl said then leaned over the rail and waved at a group of boys. The combination of being called 'the old lady' with my understanding of why Erica so badly didn't want to offend her friends forced an unbelievable statement out of my mouth.

"Or I'll go too if you'll ride with me," I squeaked.

"Will you?" Erica whispered. "I know you're scared."

"I am." I watched a family with two small children board ahead of us. The exit was now at my right. "But if you don't want to, I'm happy to bail." *Please pick bail...please pick bail.*

"Let's do it." Erica must be delusional if she thinks going with me is going to keep her safe. I had to tackle a beast I'd managed to avoid for more than half my life and I had to do it with a smile so I wouldn't scare the girl.

We climbed into the log and sat on the wet seat. A wet butt meant water would be coming in. That was okay. I didn't want anything to be going out. Erica's hands shook on my shoulders so I tried to be brave for her.

I was in the front of our two-person seat in the log.

"Check out Brer Fox." I tried to distract us both on the gently bobbing log on the narrow river. "This is so cool. I've missed it every time."

The small vignettes during the line held nothing against these large, neon-lighted story lines. Attracted to the dozens of animated animals, what was left of my stomach dropped out from underneath me with the log and I squeezed the damp metal side bar tight enough for all the bones in both wrists to crack in defiance.

"Oh shit!" Erica screamed in my ear at the moment we landed hard at the next level.

"We did it!" I cried, then frowned in the dark. We hadn't reached the big drop yet. That was on the outside of the mountain.

"Sorry about the 'shit' stuff. Oops," Erica caught herself, "sorry again. I can't believe that was so brutal and it's not even the big drop."

"That's okay. No matter what happens we will know we didn't chicken out. We did it." *Although living with poultry courage had been enough for me.*

Our log caught in the track and we ratcheted up. Notch to notch. I looked back at the girl, through the dim light I saw her green face. Her hands were squeezing the same metal hand rail. *I hope she doesn't barf on me. I hope I don't.*

"Zippidy do dah, zippidy dey"…the song grew louder. I sang. I must have been fairly ridiculous because she laughed.

"Scared?" she asked.

"To death." *If every muscle wasn't frozen I'd pee my pants.* "I won't let this ride beat me! Zippidy do—Ah!!!"

The ground dropped beneath me and a bright flash of light popped. Free falling toward a pile of man-made rocks before me, I craved gravity. We jolted to a landing and the cold water splashed on my pants and chest and I smiled large enough to make my cheeks ache. If I felt cold, I was still alive.

"Are you okay Erica?"

"Yeah," she exhaled. "How about you?"

"Brave, fearless and certain I never want to do this again in my life." Erica held up her palm and I slapped my first high five.

The log veered to the right and slowed to a stop. I turned to Erica. We looked like we'd run the Boston Marathon. Not the first place runners, but the people at the end who crawl in inch- by-inch at last place, de-hydrated muscles twitching.

Erica's friends were waiting at the exit in front of a TV screen showing photos taken of the carts during the drop. *First they scare me to death, then they take my picture?* I found our shot. We looked alike. Okay my skin was not as tight, my hair not as hip, but we had the same "I might die from this fall, but I won't let a ride stop me" face.

I bought two copies and had one sent to my room at the Castle.

"Erica" I handed her a copy. "You earned one of these. It's a rite of passage. You're living on the wild side now."

"Thank you," she called.

Exhausted and soaking wet from the waist down, I watched Erica run to catch up with her friends with the envy of the lonely. I stepped into the closest store and heard my name.

"Hey Mini," Colin said. He gave me a quick appraisal. "You don't look like you enjoyed the ride."

"That's one way to look at it," I searched past the beach towels for dry shorts in my size and tried not to think about my lack of clothing the last time he saw me.

"I thought you didn't go on that one."

"I don't. I finally found someone more scared then I was to ride that thing." Soggy and nauseous from my near-death experience, I had no patience or words to describe how I ended up taking that particular plunge. I was already sorry I'd told him about Michael yesterday. "Excuse me, but I need to change."

"Then where to?" he stood between me and the dressing room.

"Winnie the Pooh looks like my speed. Then something to eat. I left my stomach on the ride." I looked out at the crowd moving together in families and wished I had someone to share the day with.

"Well, I have work to do," he said. "Shall I call a guest services employee to escort you today?"

I'd hoped he'd gotten over worrying I would destroy the park. "That's okay. I'm used to being alone." It was true, but once it was out of my mouth, it was another thing I wished I hadn't told him. I need to practice keeping secrets. Just because I told the truth, didn't mean I had to say everything.

Chapter 17

Two churros later my stomach was settled and I glided down the elevator of the Haunted House. The safety bar closed on my lap and I rode through the ultimate after-life experience for ghosts. This was exactly where I'd want to end up if I didn't make it past purgatory. Another Protestant wanna-be place.

Dad had always liked to try to startle me in the Haunted House, tickling me in the graveyard while transparent ghosts danced around us. Mom would try to keep me calm by pointing out the pretty dresses the dancers wore or the one set of dinner dishes with an extra bread plate positioned like Mickey's head.

A vision of a bearded ghost joined me in the mirror at the exit and I wished for even Colin's company.

My earlier adrenaline was gone and I was hot in the cotton Minnie Mouse shorts that left part of my legs sticking to the ride seats.

The blanket of heat lifted when I wandered through the exit doors to the Pirates of the Caribbean, fanning myself with my Key to the Castle pass. I was greeted by the sound of the river and watched the boats returning from the Pirate adventure. It was one of my favorite rides. My people-watching skills noticed I was the only single rider among the groups of families and friends.

The line for those without fast passes was long and the boats were stacking up. But I had the Key so my wait time was a few minutes.

Three laughing women probably in their mid thirties were standing in the line for normal people. It was easy to see they were a group because they wore identical turquoise blue t-shirts that read "Disneyland is no place for children," with a large cursive B printed on the sleeve.

"How many?" The mate asked me.

"One," I mumbled.

"How many," he repeated loud enough for everyone to hear I was alone.

"Just me."

"Row One," he said, then looked to the women. "How many?"

"Four—I mean three," the women in the front said.

"Rows two and three," he pointed to my boat.

"We need our own boat," the tallest woman said. I was unwanted again.

"Sorry Ma'm," he said. "The boats are too stacked up. I have to meet the minimum." He went to the next group and the women climbed in.

"Well, we'll have to come back and try again," the tall one said.

"Are you kidding," the other woman said. "We waited an hour. I'm not sure my heart could stand that much more anticipation."

Everyone was silent and I wondered why the woman with the heart problem would be worried about this ride. No seatbelts. Even babies could ride. Even me. We loaded and I slid to the right up against the side.

One woman behind me, the other two in the next row back.

Our boat butted the boat in front and rocked to a stop waiting for the bottleneck to clear.

The women whispered and I sat silent in the front row pretending to be interested in the rows of rope piled next to the ramp and planned to ride again later alone.

Twisting on the damp bench I turned to watch the diners at the Blue Bayou restaurant. I'd never eaten at the small bistro that set along the beginning water way of Pirates, lighted by animated lightning bugs and complete with sounds of the crickets.

The boat launched off into the river that winds around the back of the restaurant and stopped again at the cabin where the same old animatronics bayou man had been rocking since I was six. I envied him. A place to go and knowing what you were doing every day. Of course I had one up on him, being alive and all.

I relaxed into my anonymity and soaked in the ride's atmosphere while we waited our turn to get moving again when my phone rang.

Damn! I grabbed at my bag.

"Hello," I whispered. The women laughed behind me at something I couldn't hear.

"I can barely hear you—repeat," Michael said.

"Hello." I rested my head on my hand, elbow on my knee. The cell coverage was slipping.

"Who's laughing?" he asked.

"It's the neighbors. They're having a party." I was going to hell for sure.

"Is the lawn ready for this week's dinner?"

At least in my mind. The boat moved and my cell phone crackled. "Almost. I've removed the brown patches. I have to go and replace the sod before it dries out."

"And don't worry about the menu," he said. "Jessica will be joining our regular group and she'll bring the food. I'll get back to you later when you're in the house." *Click.*

Jessica joined the group? He was bringing the girl he was having an affair with to our home? *My* home?

My parent's home.

I pocketed my phone then glanced back. All three women were staring at me.

"My husband," I mumbled, the fear of what had happened turned my stomach. How much longer could I say that? If I left him, I'd lose the house. The half that he'll receive anyway. Leaving me with nothing. Could I make him stop seeing her?

"That's okay," the woman behind me held out a hand—embarrassed by her friends rudeness. "I'm Katie. The tall one's Teresa. And that's Nicole."

"Mini," I shook her hand.

"So he doesn't know you're here?" Katie asked.

"No. I live about five miles away so I plan to get home tonight and get the yard work done before he returns."

"Like Beth." They all nodded. The tall one's eyes watered.

"He knows I was here yesterday, but then he had to go to Vegas for a, uh ...work trip and I decided to stay another day. What does your shirt mean?" I asked.

"After waiting in line with cranky, tired, children and husbands we decided they get in the way," Katie said. "We've been going to Disneyland together, us girls, once a year for five years."

"Sometimes we'll buy a bag of cookies to sit and people watch for an hour," Teresa added.

"Lines aren't long when you're with your friends talking," Nicole said. "And we do love to talk."

The boat dipped down a few feet beneath a skull and crossbones marked "Dead Men Tell no Tales." *I was no murderer, but if Michael died of, say, a traffic accident or an aneurism, then I'd have no problems?* "And your husbands don't care?"

"Mine's thankful he never has to come here anymore," Katie said. "Nicole's husband goes to a sports event of some kind."

"Not every husband is okay with it," Teresa added. The women nodding, somber.

"Beth's husband," Katie patted the B on her sleeve, "was reluctant at first."

"Reluctant!" They laughed.

The pirates' song and a round of a cannon battle grew so I leaned closer to hear about another woman's imperfect husband. "Okay, he didn't think they should do things apart."

"So we invited him to come along with us. The only husband allowed. After two years of following us around through every store and ride he decided one day apart a year was okay."

"What happened to Beth?" I asked, afraid to hear the answer.

"Breast cancer at thirty-five," Katie said. "She heard once that a man brought his wife's ashes to Disneyland and spread them through Pirates of the Caribbean. So we came to honor her."

"Oh?" I glanced over each bag for the shape of an urn.

"But he wouldn't hear of it. He wanted to spread her ashes over their back five acres where his will be spread someday," Teresa said.

"It was a lovely ceremony," Nicole added.

"Yes" Katie said. "Though a decidedly windy day for ash spreading."

"Yes, decidedly." Nicole smiled. The boat carried us underground to the main ride. The spray of water that covered my legs was a relief from the heat.

"Besides, cameras watch us all the way through the ride. We wouldn't want to be kicked out – though I'd love to see Disney jail," Katie said. "So we've come up with our own tribute to Beth. I'm sorry if we're a downer ride. We planned to be alone."

The boat floated through a pirate hologram into a lagoon where a battle was underway. Katie asked, "Ready?"

"You start," they pointed back to Teresa, who pulled out a square folded paper and tilted it out over the water to read.

"Everything I needed to know I learned at a Disney movie," read Teresa while the boat approached a coastal town.

Between canon blasts from an offshore pirate ship, she continued the ceremony reading from the paper in her hand, "Dumbo taught us that if you believe in yourself you can fly."

The women sniffled a bit as the boat turned into the stream leading through the pirate grotto.

Nicole took her time unfolding her notes. The boat floated in front of an animatronics man being dunked in and out of a well by pirates as his wife screamed for help from the window above. *Would I try to save Michael from pirates? Or dunk him myself?*

Nicole cleared her throat a couple of times, then read, "From Pinocchio we learned to be honest and do the right thing."

Mesmerized by the ceremony and the truth behind the lessons, I was caught off guard when a loud crack from the Pirates' scene brought me back to the ride. I was missing it. But I didn't care. I had found my herd. Of course they didn't know it, but knowing that they existed make me feel … *what was the right word?* Validated. There were other inhabitants of my fantasy bubble; other women who have fought for the right to choose their own reality. I was not alone. There might be a way I could make this happen for me. A way to have it all.

Katie leaned over the edge of the boat, trying to catch some light and then read, "From our friend Ariel who taught us to find your own place in the world."

"Not to mention more than a shellful is a waste!" laughed Katie.

A pirate was slouched against a barrel where a Johnny Depp lookalike peeked out. There used to be a woman in the barrel when it was created in 1972, I remembered seeing it when I was a kid before it was updated to a cat, then a version of Captain Jack Sparrow. *I still feel like the woman peeking out to see if the man is gone so I can run to my life.*

High wooden beams, burning in orange embers overhead cracked and threatened to drop on both the boats and the chaos of pirate-looting on each side of the waterway.

"Hurry up," Nicole said to Teresa in the back who unfolded another square of paper. "We still have three more and we're already near the ramp."

Teresa leaned over and read "Thank you Snow White for showing that if you run away your problems will follow."

Katie rushed through her part. "To Sleeping Beauty who taught us not to sleep through life. A kiss may not wake you up, but it can sure feel good."

The boat passed a pirate sleeping with the pigs…his twitching toes showed his happiness when Nicole read the last note. "From the Swiss Family Robinson: Family matters the most."

We floated for a moment with only the sounds of the ride. Katie tapped me on the shoulder. "Thank you for putting up with us."

"No problem. It was beautiful." I turned to the next scene to give them privacy and came face-to-animated-face with another Johnny Depp. I thought I saw a twinkle in his waxy eye. Even in the costume of a scallywag, I wanted to climb up on his lap as he rocked back and forth greeting the departing passengers. "Is it okay if I say something for Beth?"

"Sure," Katie patted my hand.

"Disney's most interesting lesson," I said. *I missed not just being wanted, but wanting.* "Johnny Depp makes a totally hot pirate!"

Nicole snorted loud enough for the passengers in the boat waiting on the ramp in front of us to turn around.

"You fit right in," Katie laughed. "Beth would have loved you."

It was so beautiful to see that some women have friends to celebrate each other's lives. And so wonderful that they shared a similar love for the park. And so sad that I'd never known this type of friendship.

One of Katie's papers had slipped to the floor of the boat so I bent to pick it up then I climbed out. The three women had already moved onto the dock and were whispering again.

I walked past them, intending to hand the note and walk on when Katie grabbed my arm.

"We've decided that we'd love for you to join our Disney club," she said.

"Club?" I muttered.

"We meet once a week at my house for coffee, then once or twice a year we all come together," Katie said. "You've been unanimously nominated for membership! That is if you'd like to?"

Was she kidding? I'd almost jumped overboard and decided to live in the Pirates of the Caribbean for the rest of my life because I had no future. I could share the park with friends. Of course it would never work, but there was a joy in being wanted.

Katie handed me her phone and I entered my number. Then the lanyard holding my pass slipped out of my top.

"You're the one!" Katie gasped and reached to touch the key. "I heard somebody won yesterday! Girls— she's the grand prize winner."

All three women blocked the exit each asking to see and touch the Key to the Castle.

"You get to stay in the castle? Oh that must be wonderful." Nicole said.

I wished I could invite them up to see it. But I didn't think I was supposed to have visitors. But then what could the Disney Police do to me? Ruin my marriage?

Make me lose my parent's home? I'd already done the worst to myself.

"Come with me and I'll show you," the words came out of my mouth like a normal polite woman being courteous to a group of new friends. Or like a woman desperate for any shreds of friendship.

We moved out into New Orleans Square and I handed Katie the paper I'd found. In the bright lights of late afternoon I saw that the page was blank. Except for a light dust of ash.

Chapter 18

Happy to be part of a small herd, I led my new friends through Fantasyland to the secret wooden door at the base of the Castle. I made a large ceremony out of opening it and waving them up the spiral staircase.

"Oh my God, I can't believe it!" Teresa ran to the large window of my Castle room and waved out. "Can they see me? It must be one-way glass."

"It's so wonderful," Katie gasped.

"And check out the bar." Nicole pulled the door open. It was stuffed with treats and drinks. "It says help yourself, all complimentary.

I hadn't even gone behind the bar to see what was there, let alone if it was free. I could have saved myself a trip downstairs as the queen this morning if I'd seen that bag of salty corn chips and dark chocolate bar. Teresa pulled out a bottle of champagne.

"Shall we?" she asked.

I wasn't a drinker. Michael hasn't touched a drink since his DUI. He believed it clouded your judgment. I hoped he was right. Right now I wanted to fog things up. "You bet."

In half a minute I had two glasses from the sideboard, a coffee mug, and one plastic cup from the bathroom each filled with champagne.

"To Mini," Katie said. "Thanks for the great tour!"

125

"To Beth," I said. "Thanks for introducing me to your friends."

Everyone settled on the massive bed slumber-party style and talked at once. The champagne was sweet and tickled at the same time. *I do like it.*

"I dreamed about winning this," Katie admitted. "Imagine having a lifetime pass at all the Disney parks in the world. And a trip around the world to visit each park and a Disney cruise…"

"What?" I choked and wiped the champagne off my chin that didn't make it down my throat. I'd always wanted to travel, but Michael had no interest past golfing in Palm Springs or Vegas and then always by himself. Or so I'd thought.

"It's been all over the local papers. Haven't you seen the ads?"

"No." *How foolish I must look to not even remember what I'd won.* "They went over all this with me yesterday, but I don't remember the details."

"Oh there's so much more," Katie said. "Didn't you have to sign some paperwork or something?"

I scrambled for the prize package and dumped it out on the bed. My new friends and I poured through the paperwork to the travel section—still unsigned.

"I can't believe I forgot," I finished my glass and poured another, passing the bottle around until it was empty and I'd thought of what to say that wouldn't increase my standing as an idiot. Cashing in the travel part of the prize could help me buy Michael out of the house.

"I live about eight miles away in La Habra," Katie said. "There must be four billboards between here and there announcing the Key to the Castle."

126

How big a hermit have I been?

"Honestly I was overwhelmed when I won," I added, deciding not to share the fact that it was the sight of Michael kissing Jessica that had pushed me over the edge. "I don't remember much about the first hours after. I'm supposed to decide on the travel or the cash before I leave."

"Are you happy Mini?" Katie asked.

"Happy? I don't know. I guess. Since my parents died I've kept busy enough not to miss them. Happiness wasn't something I tried to reach."

"Wow you're deep. I meant the prize," Katie laughed.

"Uh, yeah." *Gotta work on that sharing without sharing thing.*

"So what is up with your husband?" Katie asked. "Why isn't he here?"

What do I care if I tell these women my pathetic story? I took a long drink. "I found out yesterday that he is having an affair with a young girl he works with. They're at a convention in Vegas right now."

"Does he know?" Teresa gasped and I shook my head. "What are you going to do?"

That was a good question, but not one that I had an answer for yet. "I don't know. If we can fix it, he's probably my last chance to have a family. If not, I'll need to stay at least until I figure out how to make a living. I'm not sure I'm that good a secret keeper."

"I could never do that," Nicole said. "I'd tear his hair out and then take him for all he's got."

"It's up to Mini," Katie said. "Remember this is her life. It's her choice what she wants to do. Even if her choice is nothing."

127

"Thanks, I haven't had this support in a long time," I rubbed at the tears in my eyes and touched my nose, "or had my nose go numb from the champagne."

Another bottle and several life stories later someone knocked at the door.

"It's the coppers! I knew we'd end up in Disney jail!" Katie laughed.

"You are obsessed!" Nicole added.

Laughter filled the entire room when I opened the door to face Colin. "You might be right after all, Katie," I said.

Colin took in the pile of women on the bed and the empty bottle of champagne resting on its side on the floor. "Felicity couldn't make it to take you to the Golden Horseshoe and asked me to fill in."

"I was just showing some people," I looked back at the women trying to look respectable, "my new friends—the Castle room. Is that okay?"

"Certainly," he drawled. "But no photos."

Katie dropped her camera back into her purse.

"How about one?" I asked. I wanted a souvenir of this moment. Proof that there was life. "You take it of all of us."

Colin cracked a rare smile he must save for park guests and held out his hand. "I don't see any harm in taking one without a view of the room."

We piled back in the bed and Colin took a quick shot. "We do have to be going Mini," he said. "The Golden Horseshoe Review is on a set schedule and the camera crew is already setting up."

"Ah, the price of fame," Katie giggled. "Come on girls, we have our own schedule to keep. Mini," she handed me a card. "Here's my work number. See you next Wednesday at my house."

Teresa gave Colin the once over as she passed him. "You're real cute."

I opened my mouth to shush her when a loud burp that started at my knees erupted. I couldn't believe I'd done that in front of everyone—especially Colin. I would add that to the list of things to pretend I didn't do.

"Or maybe we'll go to California Adventure for some champagne!" They all laughed their way out of the room, each one giving me a hug and her phone number.

I watched them walk off together, honored to be a small temporary part of their group. I missed friends. I didn't even know where any of my pre-Michael friends were. *When did that happen? In my darkness?*

"Are you okay to be on film?" Colin asked when the door closed.

"Aren't you getting tired of asking me that?" I picked up the bottle.

"Yes, I am," he took the empty champagne bottle and dropped it into the trash. "Do yourself a favor and down a bottle of water or two. Then meet me downstairs in about ten minutes?"

"I'm fi—rrraa." I burped. Judging by the amount of heat in my cheeks, I must've been as red as Mickey's shorts.

Chapter 19

Smirking, dagger-eyes or disapproval were among the looks I was prepared for from Colin when I opened the bottom door to venture back into Fantasyland. The unexpected smile that went all the way to his eyes made me blush to the tips of my Minnie sandals.

"How about we pretend the stair incident never occurred?" I offered. "And while we're at it, everything embarrassing that's happened to me since I arrived yesterday."

"Whatever you say," Colin waved his hand forward. "Let's pretend. Your majesty."

While I'm at it, I'll pretend that Disneyland is my home. And that I am a happy woman. No one else has to know the truth.

"You don't have to do anything special. Billy will introduce you," Colin said on our walk to the Golden Horseshoe Review in Frontierland. "I won't make the same mistake as yesterday and assume you won't want to make a comment. But if it involves a potential riot please give me some warning."

The lightness in his voice sounded like he was smiling, but I was still too self conscious for direct eye contact. The bubbles that had tickled my nose earlier found their way to my feet. I was skipping. I stopped short and held my hands up.

131

"I don't plan to do anything but enjoy the show," I said. "All the times I visited with my parents I've never been to the review."

"You're in for a real treat then. Billy has been here for more years then I can remember. It's a great rest stop to put a load in your belly and laugh the calories away."

"You sound like a tour guide." I inhaled the scent of popcorn as we passed the cart where the same young man was still working. I stopped for a box and to say hello.

We walked the short distance between the Castle and Frontierland and onto the long porch in front of the shops connected to the Golden Horseshoe Review. I let the joy of the park mingle with the last remnants of the champagne. I had friends.

"Hi Min, sorry I'm late," Peter met us on the front porch and squeezed me into a surprise hug. I held on extra long, thinking of that huge bed back in my Castle. Was there anything I could use as a lure?

My brain told me that I was trying to get even with Michael. My body told my brain to shut the hell up.

"I worked on a little something for you," Peter said.

"I didn't think I'd see you again."

Colin made a scratchy sound deep in his throat that reminded me I was not alone. "Do you know Colin?" I asked Peter who was already shaking Colin's hand.

"Sure, you were on the last job performance review I had," he said. "Thanks for the raise, by the way."

"You do a great job," Colin grimaced. *A funny face to make when someone was thanking you.* "How do you know Mini?"

132

"From the parade. But actually we got to know each other last night when she helped me with the gardening outside the Castle," he gave me a bright smile that made me want to have my teeth whitened. I was thrilled that I'd chosen the lower cut top to wear. If I'm going to hell in a hand basket, I wanted someone to think I was pretty…desirable.

"You don't have to be doing chores while you're our guest here," Colin's familiar frown had returned.

I didn't want Peter to be in trouble because of me. "That's okay. It was fun." Planting flowers with a prince was not a common occurrence, but Colin didn't have to know what a bumbling klutz I had been.

"Yeah and she has a real gift with pansies," Peter added.

Probably because I am one. "You did say I could make myself at home and do what I want."

"That I did. Thank you for your help," Colin looked at his watch. "Well, since you have someone to enjoy the show with and I have something I should see to, I'll leave you with Peter."

"She's in good hands mate," Colin's eyes followed Peter's hand at my waist.

"Thank you Colin," I called, but he'd already turned away. Peter guided me toward my seat.

We walked past the food counter, and a cake almost tall enough to dance with, to a box seat on stage right. I sat in one of the two white iron chairs at a small round table. I waved to the familiar camera crew set up in the balcony and watched as line of guests began filling the room. *Why in the world would Peter want to spend this time with me?*

133

"What would you like to eat?" a waitress dressed as a saloon girl asked.

I leaned over the rail to try to see the menu on the wall. "What do you have?"

"Oh they have the best stuff," Peter said. "Let me order for you and you tell me if I got it right?"

"Okay," Michael always ordered for me. Double what he wanted. This was practical since I never finished a meal and he could eat the extra.

"Two of everything, except one of the mile-high cake," Peter ordered. "I don't know about your chocolate appetite, but it's way too big for me to eat a whole one."

"I do have a large appetite," I met his eyes for a brief bold second before I chickened out. Flirting was hard work and took a courage I didn't seem to have. Yet.

"I can tell," he smiled.

The house lights dimmed to fade some of the warm blush on my face.

Billy's stage entrance started a round of applause. The show promised to be something between vaudeville and Grand Ole Opry meets Southern California.

Piles of food were delivered to our table and Peter moved his chair around to sit next to me, his hand on the back of my chair. I decided to be coy and stuffed chicken tenders into my mouth.

"Have you decided to dump your husband yet?" he whispered.

Gasping with your mouth full was a no-win situation. The food was either coming out in a sputter or going down too fast and cutting off your air supply.

Unfortunately instead of choking to death, what was left of my chicken nugget came out into my hand as I coughed.

He patted my back in tender circles while I tried to clear the debris with my napkin. "Are you okay?"

I nodded. "Give me a warning next time you want to ask such a personal question so you don't startle me to death."

"Okay. Warning!" He used his napkin and cleaned something off my chin. "You know there's something about you that makes me want to make sure you're happy. Don't you want to be? You're so…"

The fiddling grew louder and I tapped a finger to my ear in a sign that I couldn't hear what he said. A flash of guilt washed over me as I thought of the yard work left undone and the sex I'd like to have with this cute stranger. I stuffed myself with food to keep from spilling my lust.

"They're good," I mumbled as the music volume dropped at the end of the song.

"Yeah! They've been doing this for twenty years. I've been trying to get on stage with them since I was seventeen but they say I don't fit the hillbilly image!"

"We'll, you are more J. Crew than overalls." Although I'd love to see him in a pair; one side unbuckled, front flap hanging sideways, with one nipple and a few cans from his six or eight pack peeking out.

"I know," he smiled. He didn't need false modesty. "But I always loved this little stage."

The band restarted. As they fiddled, sang and told jokes I tried to act normal, but couldn't remember what

135

that was. Then the largest piece of chocolate cake was placed before me and the rest of the world went black.

I sunk my fork into the inside of the wedge and scooped out a hunk of one of the seven layers. The center frosting melted over my tongue and I chewed on the chunks of chocolate chips. Peter sunk his fork into the point at one end and I caught myself before stabbing him with my utensil to protect every morsel. It was cake made to share.

"That's the way to eat cake," Peter leaned his elbow on the table and watched my indulgence.

"Stop staring." I wiped the chocolate off my teeth with my tongue.

The music stopped for a moment and Billy spoke.

"Thank you," he said, waving to the crowd. "Our CD is for sale next door. If you buy it will you make us a copy?" The crowd roared as he continued. "So we have a grand prize winner with us today. Mini Gunderson."

I waved my hand and smiled to the crowd without standing up. *I will not start a riot today.*

"I heard from a little birdie that you're a country music fan," Billy said. "Know any Charlie Daniel's?"

"Yes," I wiped what I hoped was the last of the frosting off my mouth, kicking Peter under the table. "I'd love to hear you sing one."

"We are. Come up and sing a song with us."

"Oh no—" I laughed. "I promised to stay out of trouble today."

"This is my surprise." Peter pulled me up. "You'll be great."

"There's no way I can do this alone," I said. But then again, why not? "Not without Peter."

"Come on up then!"

I let Peter lead me up to the microphone. "Hi," I squeaked to the audience that looked relieved to be sitting inside in the air conditioning on a hot late afternoon. Billy started on the guitar with the Hillbillies on the fiddle.

"I'll start and you take over." Billy sang in a long clear voice, "The devil went down to Georgia, he was looking for a soul to steal…he was in a bind 'cuz he was way behind."

Peter pointed to me and I sang to him: "My name is Johnny, chicken in the bread pin picking out dough…"

"Wait, wait, wait," Billy waved his fiddle and bow in the air. "Now Mini, I can hear you have a voice. But we've gotta reach those folks up in the balcony so let go of those pipes."

I shook my head. That was a long way up there.

"Help her get the courage," he said to the audience.

The crowd clapped and I smiled as my ego reawakened. The sea of vacationing faces waited. They were here to have fun. I had nothing left to lose.

"The devil went down to Georgia," Peter and Billy started again.

"Ah oooo!" I surprised everyone—including myself—when I hit the note I hadn't reached for years, even in the shower. Billy's eyebrows raised up into his cowboy hat.

The clapping increased and we sang louder. My inner ham hadn't been out of the barn in a long time and it loved the sunshine. *I am invincible.*

Billy's partner fiddled his heart out playing both parts of the duet. We clapped along with the audience who howled. Peter bowed and I dropped into the same

137

curtsey I'd learned at the end of "The King and I" my freshman year.

I spotted Colin standing on the side and had to will myself on. He wouldn't be happy.

Only, the look on his face wasn't anger, frustration or the placating look you give to a mental patient. It was, dare I say it, admiration? No, it couldn't be. Not from him.

Peter picked up the beginning of the next song and took my hand. I joined in. The audience stood up at the middle of the song on tired 'I've-been-waiting-in-lines-all-morning' feet and clapped along.

"They love your music," I said to Billy over the applause at the end.

"They love you," Billy laughed. "I'm pretty jealous."

A tug at my clothes brought my attention to a little girl at the edge of the stage.

"Will you sign my autograph book?" she asked. When I had imagined this moment—when I had imagination—I never pictured it filling me with such joy. To be appreciated doing something I loved.

She opened her book to a blank page across from Mickey's signature and I signed.

Lost in ego-inflating appreciation, I floated down the steps to the floor level and forgot the right step in the left, right, left part of walking, and slipped. I reached out with my right hand to stop my fall and knocked a plate of chocolate cake out of a woman's hand into the chest of Colin.

And then there it was—the disapproving look I'd expected to see earlier.

"I'm sorry," I called as Peter and I were ushered out the side door by the stern-faced—and chocolate-chested—park director. "I don't know why these things happen to me."

"This way," Colin led us through the kitchen with one hand on my arm.

"I feel like Elvis." I said to the two new men in my life.

"I'd say you're closer to Lucille Ball," Colin said, his other hand wiping cake off his jacket. He walked to the clam chowder station and took a rag to clean up.

Peter squeezed my hand. "We're great together! You're my good luck charm. I got to sing onstage with Billy! Around you anything's possible. I'd love to hang with you some more, but I have to work Toon Town for a Goofy who called in sick."

"That's okay. I'm going on some rides." I was still high from being on stage and wanted to continue floating for a while.

"Want to go for a walk after my shift?" Peter asked. "The park is reopening for a corporate event."

Peter hugged me and I inhaled his scent, musky. *Hmm. A great smelling guy friend who hugs. I can stand that.*

"You make friends fast," Colin watched me watch Peter walk away.

"Not usually. Or ever," I shrugged. But I was up to, what? Three women, a couple of teenagers, a fairy godmother and one hot prince. I had seven friends.

"We have something in common then," Colin said. "Where to?"

"I'll take a walk."

139

"I'll stick with you for a while." We strolled down to the water and watched a group of guests climbing into the canoe ride before he spoke. "You're a good singer."

"No, but thanks."

"Have you been on stage a lot?"

"Not since college, the first year that is."

We walked along the water next to the split rail fence, avoiding the crowds.

"I meant to tell you earlier," Colin said, "Felicity wants to join you for dinner. She'll meet you at the Castle later."

"Great." We passed the entrance to the Winnie the Pooh ride and I stopped to stare into the barn front. "What happened to the Country Bear Jamboree?"

"They've added another ride for the little ones outside of Fantasyland," he said.

"Oh," I whined. "I looked forward to watching Teddi Barra drop from the ceiling on her flower-covered swing."

"I miss it too," Colin said. "Though my favorite bear was Henry."

"That's because you're a guy," I stopped at the entrance of a candy store. "I'll go pick out a few treats. Don't worry. I won't start any riots."

Already on the phone, he waved as I turned.

So much I didn't know, but the marshmallows on a stick displayed in the window appeared to be dipped into both caramel and dark chocolate and deserved all my attention.

Chapter 20

Normally the mad scramble of the last few minutes before the park closes for the day draws crowds of people toward the front, emptying the park from the back. Except for the final rides in Fantasyland, most of the exhausted people—having spent twelve or more hours on their feet—could be found packed into the many shops of Main Street trying to find that perfect something that would remind them of their day in the park.

It was a little different when the park closed early at seven. Energies were still high, all the money hadn't been spent and there was still enough energy to try to race to each land and grab a quick ride before being ushered out.

The flow of people led me from land to land for about an hour as I soaked in their excitement and laid out my options.

I could stay with Michael and pretend I didn't see a thing and let life go on until I figured out my path. If I did, I'd come to the park every weekday while he was at work either with my new friends or alone.

Confront Michael—the other option. That would end one of two ways. He could fall on his knees, beg for forgiveness and make me an equal part of his life, or he could leave me. That would speed up the 'need to find a

141

job, home and car' exponentially. And depending on the job I could find, I might never have time to come to the park and enjoy my lifetime prize. I was no closer to figuring out what to do, but I had circled around Fantasyland and was back to the Castle door.

I entered across the drawbridge to make it to my door through the crowds. I wished I could have brought them all up to see my beautiful room.

The suite was quiet compared to the afternoon with my new friends. I dressed for dinner with Felicity—the closest to a fairy godmother a girl from Anaheim Hills could expect. I'd be at the park fewer than another twenty hours and I wanted to enjoy every minute.

And I may have a date with a prince. Granted, he was just being nice and liked to hang out with me for some reason. But I liked the idea.

I took a quick shower, pulled my hair into a headband and slipped on a powder blue sundress with Daisy Duck trim. The innocent print was balanced by a tight bodice that best showed off the shape of my breasts. I was going out fully loaded.

Leaving my large bag in the room, I grabbed my new shell purse, Minnie lipstick and the pass.

I opened the door to Colin who was raising his hand, about to knock.

"Hey," I mumbled.

"Felicity couldn't make it. One of her grandchildren is pitching tonight."

Energy drained out of my limbs and I slumped in the doorway.

"I was looking forward to it," I said. "But I can grab something."

"Felicity asked me to step in, and I'm starving." Colin said. He had changed too—the fresh shirt under his traditional jacket was the same shade of blue as my dress.

"We look like prom dates," I laughed.

"I should have brought a corsage!" He laughed. I couldn't tell if he was warming up to me or happy that I hadn't caused any scenes in the last hour.

"You don't have to do this," I tried to sound more secure than usual. "Just because Felicity couldn't come, you know. I can have something brought up."

"You're not hungry? That's a first," he frowned. "Or you don't want to spend the evening with me?"

"Yes. I mean yes, I'm hungry. I don't want you to have to entertain me tonight. You've already put in a full day on the job," but I didn't want to be alone anymore. I'd experienced a quick taste of friends and liked it.

"My work day never ends. The night crew is getting the park ready for the new batch," Colin smiled and I relaxed. "But I'm starved. Let's go have a nice dinner."

The park guests had been cleared out of Fantasyland, but a congestion of strollers and visitors bottle-necked at the front of Main Street.

A group of white swans and two black swans had gathered near the drawbridge as we passed over.

"They are so beautiful," I stopped and leaned over the thick rail watching them swim under the bridge. "Where have they been all day?"

"They hide from the sun and the visitors. They come out here every night for feeding, then rush off when the park reopens."

The last white tail disappeared under the bridge and I ran to the other side and watched them glide out. "Who has the park tonight?"

"A Japanese auto company. We'll reopen for them in a couple of hours."

I loved being in the park after dark. And I was hungry. "So where are we eating? What's open?"

"Club 33."

I stopped in my tracks and grabbed his tight, muscular arm. "You're kidding! I've always wanted to see the secret club."

"It's no secret," Colin laughed, his smile easy. "But there is a ten-year waiting list for membership. Of course it's part of your prize, so you won't ever have to worry about it."

A lifetime eating at Club 33 in Disneyland. That would be quite a cafeteria. If I only had a job and a place to live, leaving Michael might be an option.

Skipping on the inside, and I hoped walking calmly on the outside, we traveled through Adventureland to a small door in New Orleans square. We were buzzed into the entry at the foot of a large staircase. A golden elevator carried us up one floor and my imagination through the roof.

Past dark paneled walls and a full bar, we were shown to a table for two by a tuxedo-dressed waiter. The view through the shutters overlooked the Blue Bayou Restaurant and I saw the fireflies dancing over the river on the Pirates of the Caribbean lobby. I couldn't help but think of my new friends. They would love this. I'd have to find out if I could bring them with me.

144

The waiter handed me a menu. "Definitely chocolate mousse," I read from the bottom up.

"Your eyes go right to the dessert," Colin smiled. "What about dinner?"

"I have no idea," I put down the menu. "Order whatever you think is good."

Colin picked it up and handed it back to me. "You take all the time you need and we'll order whatever you want." He leaned back in his chair and motioned to the waiter to open a bottle of champagne.

The light tinkle of glasses in the background, combined with the soft piano music, surrounded me and while Colin spoke to several staff members and had a couple of brief radio calls, I took the time to choose exactly what I wanted to eat. Almost one of everything.

"Champagne?" he asked after I had ordered. "Or have you had enough today?"

"You know, I never drink, or not until today, but I do like champagne." I handed over my glass and watched the bubbles fill to the rim.

Colin leaned forward and whispered, "So do I, but don't tell anyone. I don't want to lose my macho image."

"With your shoulders, you have no fear of that," I leaned back against the chair, no longer afraid of what might come out of my mouth. "I thought you hated me."

"Why?" He reached out his hand as if to take mine, then stopped short.

The bubbles on the second sip no longer tickled my nose, and I hoped they wouldn't start me burping again. "Well, then let's say you thought I'd bring Disneyland down all by myself."

"That's true," his laughter was deep and mellow. "But you seem different today too. That was quite a show this afternoon."

My face must have matched the red of the radish cut in the silhouette of my favorite mouse that topped the salad placed in front of me. "I'm sorry again about the cake on your jacket. I didn't plan on getting up on stage."

"I know. That's what made it so good. You have a terrific singing voice."

I didn't know if it was the champagne or the compliments but my heart beat a little faster. I relived the thrill of being accepted on the stage. "Thanks. I wasn't sure I remembered how."

"Why?"

I poured the thick French dressing over the lettuce as I took my time answering. "I don't know. I guess my husband likes things quiet."

We ate for a few minutes in silence and I thought of a way to explain Michael. I found no words. I couldn't even explain myself.

"Your husband sounds a bit..." Colin paused long enough for me think of ways to fill in the blank: *cheating, always right.* but his choice was "forceful?" Then it dawned on me. Colin was asking if my husband abused me. How many other people who met us thought that?

"No. But he is decisive and I'm not. So I let him decide everything," I said and let a bite of onion and tomato linger in my mouth before chewing. "My parents died and he took over. I never asked for control back."

"I know you had quite a shock yesterday." The entrees arrived and I busied myself with the pepper mill. "Why are you embarrassed when he's the one who did something wrong?"

If I were a better wife he wouldn't have cheated. Did I actually believe it? I shrugged and listened to the pianist.

"I'm sorry, that was way too personal," he added.

"I don't mind." I was burned out from all the lies to Michael. Opening up helped let some of the bad karma out. "What do you want to know? My life is an open book."

"What are you going to do?"

I shrugged. "He'll call again tonight. When he can't reach me at the house, he'll call my cell. I guess I'll know what I'm going to say when it comes out of my mouth."

Delivery of our entrees and small talk over the proper combination of butter versus sour cream took my life off center stage for a while.

"How about work?" Colin asked. "What do you do?"

"I take care of things for Michael. I was in school forever but there was always a reason I couldn't finish. Not meant to be I guess. I mean I do have lots of time." I pushed my empty plate to the side and leaned forward, surprised I had managed to polish it off when he had not finished his.

"But," I added, "I have no confidence. Everything I started, I stopped before finishing. I spent one year in a teaching program, two years in nursing, one year in theatre arts and two years in psychology, all with an

147

incomplete Spanish minor, a concentration in French and absolutely no degree."

He took a large bite of his dessert and I watched him chew with strong jaws. "So let's talk about the prize. What's been your favorite part of the Key to the Castle so far?"

"Knowing that I could come here whenever I wanted," I said. "I do love helping others and the atmosphere here is one of sharing. Everyone wants the dream 'Disneyland day' and wants to make sure everyone else has it too. You're so lucky to work here."

Colin nodded and sat back to finish his dessert with one hand while he answered a text with the other. Alone for a moment with my own dessert, I relished each morsel.

The last smear of chocolate was swiped off my plate and made it to my tongue when Colin finally put his phone back into his pocket and asked "Want to walk?"

"Yes," I rubbed my full stomach. "If I can."

Chapter 21

The lights sparkled off the colorful beads hanging from the balconies in New Orleans Square as we walked through the empty park.

The hours we'd spent at dinner had flown and now a crew of cleaners sprinkled the streets and alleys. The warm magic of the park soaked into me. We walked around the backside of Thunder Mountain. *This is peace.*

"So you know so much about me, but we haven't talked about you yet," I said. "Like what the E. stands for."

Colin smiled. "Well, I'm unmarried. I've worked for Disneyland for fifteen years. I started my junior year in college. In two years I worked in every department. After I graduated they hired me full time."

"And the E.?"

"I've trusted one person with that information," he said. "And it didn't work out well."

"Trust issues, huh?" I gave his shoulder a light shove. "Why didn't you ever marry?"

"I'm glad we're not letting this get too personal."

I laughed out loud. "You've known me for a day and have already seen me at my worst. You know what happened to my parents, that I have no job skills, am a

149

klutz and that my husband is cheating on me as we speak."

"Fair enough," he said. "I was married once. She didn't want kids and she didn't like the hours. If I was going to work twenty-four by seven, she wanted me to be more ambitious. Move up higher into corporate."

"But that wouldn't work for a Disney addict like you," I stopped in front of the turtle pond that was dark enough to reflect the moonlight. "Corporate means less contact with the park crowd."

"How did you figure it out that fast?" he asked. "It took her four years."

"That's how I would feel if I was lucky enough to have your job history." I couldn't believe someone would leave Colin. Not a caretaker of such wonder. "You get to play for a living."

Colin shook his head and leaned against the rail next to me. He didn't speak for several minutes. Long enough for me to start feeling uncomfortable.

He turned to face me. Close enough for me to wish I'd used the Minnie Mouse deodorant from the bathroom counter.

"It's all work now," he said. "I can't remember the last time I played."

I turned and looked up at the horizon at the top of Thunder Mountain against the starless Orange County night sky.

"I love the energy the park creates," he added. "Fun, excitement, fear, and trauma: as you saw this morning, it's always something and I love being a part of it."

"So you climbed to the highest peak at the park and hung on." I wanted to hold his hand. To be wanted. A reaction, I was sure of being deemed inadequate by one man. I walked toward a tree lighted by thousands of tiny twinkles. We passed a large picnic area full of vacant tables.

"This part of the park once had a live play of Hunchback of Notre Dame," Colin's tour guide voice took over.

"I remember Festival of Fools 1996-98," I watched Colin's jaw drop. "It was great. I probably saw it five or six times."

"Now it's used for a daily barbeque and where we handle the corporate dining events," Colin said, pointing to a rise in the landscaping. "And the Sky Buckets were right here."

"Yes and that building," I pointed to the corner shop housing hats next to the German food, "used to hold a charming store where you could design your own dolls. My mom bought me a lovely doll that had straight brown hair and eyes the color of mine. I had a bad time during puberty not fitting in. It seemed all the girls had long curly hair, so mom had the doll maker created one with short, straight, brown hair. It didn't matter that I wasn't playing with toys anymore. That doll made me feel pretty. And that spot," I said when we passed the heraldry store, "former villain's shop."

"Don't tell me. Maleficent is your favorite villain." Colin said.

"Nope. Ursula." I said.

"The Octopus?"

"Sure, she's creepy. Mean, evil, smells awful on shore I'm sure. But while Malificent is always evil, Ursula is perfectly evil. She prays on Ariel's insecurities and uses them to her advantage which in my book makes her truly evil," I smiled at the crew polishing the brass at the Dumbo ride.

Colin moved to stand face to face. "You look the happiest when you talk about Disneyland."

"It's my favorite subject. Always has been." I elbowed his ribs and I walked around him. "I am different today. I believe in Disneyland and in the possibility of happily ever after. I'm not sure how it applies to me yet."

"I get it."

"You really do." I reached up and touched his shoulder, craving physical contact with another human. "You're like my husband, but in a good way. Totally into the company and what would make it better. Disney is something special that should be protected at all costs. I wished I had somewhere I belonged."

I plopped down on a bench near the opening to Monstro the Whale.

"Are you tired?" he asked.

"Not much." I stretched my arms wide. "I'm soaking in the park. Yesterday I was too caught up in drama to enjoy it."

"Want to go on a ride?"

I looked about the empty park. Open only to me.

"Yes, but you pick. I know what I would like, but wouldn't make a grown man go with me. It can be quite painful for some people."

"This is your day."

"You asked for it. I want to go on It's a Small World." I waited to see him wince but instead he broke into a huge grin.

"You don't mean that you're going to make me go on Walt Disney's masterful recreation built for the 1964

152

Worlds' Fair? That depicts not only the hope that the countries of the world work together in harmony but was also the first generation of animatronics after the original Abraham Lincoln in 1964. What a terrible imposition."

"I didn't expect a man to want to go on this ride," we walked through the open spiral queue to the front. "Especially one who has probably been on this ride as a work requirement."

"As long as that song doesn't get stuck in my head. I do appreciate all the rides. Each one tells a story of the growth of the park."

A lone employee started up the ride when he saw the boss.

We sat in our own boat sized for sixteen. I used my cell phone to take photos of many of the dancing dolls and walked off the ride humming.

Colin stopped to call in some needed repair work he noticed on the mermaid while I waited for the first batch of popcorn from the cart near the merry-go-round, almost ready for reopening.

"I heard old Abe was out of the park for a while. Where was he?" I asked later when we circled through the front of Main Street, taking the long walk back to the Castle.

"Like all the pieces of our past exhibits he was in the Disney vault," his voice dropped low to share his secret.

"That I want to see."

"Sorry, not even with your Key to the Castle can you get in," he said. "Employees only."

153

"So if Dan Brown decided to investigate the Disneyland basement he'd find the secret that would save the world?"

"Something like that," Colin laughed. "You know, you're a lot of fun to be with."

"Never a dull moment?"

"You could say that. But I have to admit that your instincts are better than most people's well thought-out plans."

"Thank you." We walked back to the Castle in a pleasant silence.

"Thank you for a nice time," Colin said at the Castle door as he held out his hand and shook mine. "I enjoyed dinner."

"Me too," I didn't want the handshake or the night to end. "Want to come up for a night cap? I can have hot chocolate here in five minutes."

"I should go," Colin's smile told me he'd rather stay. "I have to meet the camera crew out front before the park reopens. I do hope that you and your husband work things out so that you're happy."

Oh yeah, I'm married.

Chapter 22

I pushed the door open and stopped pretending that I would leave Disneyland even one minute sooner than I had to.

"I may be a complete idiot," I said to the empty room that gave me the strongest sense of being home since mom and dad's death, "but even Colin has warmed up."

I dropped my purse and phone on the bed and was drawn out onto the balcony. I leaned on the rail munching my salty snack while watching the night crew finish final preps before reopening.

Colin stood on the drawbridge with the film crew on the right. Peter knelt at the deep purple bed of pansies on my left—cleaning up his cart, about finished. He would be at my door soon. Just as I knew I'd have to be on the phone with Michael first.

Something clicked behind me. It took a moment before I focused on the sound and realized what it meant. My breath caught in my throat as I whipped around and grabbed at the door. Too late. Locked. The park had reopened. Before I had a chance to exhale, my cell phone rang. On the wrong side of the door.

"I am in so much trouble!" I cried, my fingers pulling on the handle, trying to pry the door open. The ringing stopped and I looked down at Colin. If I called, he'd hear, but so would the camera crew. I wouldn't

155

want them to see I was in another mess. Besides, he'd just stopped thinking I was insane moments ago.

Peter was close enough to hear me call, but then Colin would too. *Think Mini!*

If I waited, Peter would know I hadn't opened the door and would come looking for me for our walk around the park tonight. Or maybe think I was blowing him off? He doesn't have a pass key that would get him up into the Castle. I still had my pass around my neck. If I caught his attention I could toss it to him and he could rescue me. Again.

My phone rang again minutes later increasing my panic. Colin was chatting with the camera crew, going over notes on a clipboard and showing no signs of leaving. Peter piled the empty flats onto his cart. He'd be gone any minute.

I used the only tool I had.

The first kernel of popcorn I tossed toward Peter fell short. I didn't have enough room. And it was damned hard to reach any distance with the light puffs.

A flow of fresh guests approached from Main Street. I needed a launcher. In a move combining Tom Sawyer and Becky Thatcher, I pulled off my headband and slung popcorn at the Prince. After five or six quick shots my aim improved and soon I was sending off multiple rounds. The kernels that fell short landed in the water.

As my aim improved, the edible ammunition inched closer to the Prince. So did the swans. They gobbled up the nibbles in a frenzy of feathers and water. Peter turned around and smiled at the large birds. Two gutsy swans climbed out onto the edge and started nibbling at the popcorn and his shoelaces.

"Help!" Holding his hands up in the air to keep his fingers out of the line of fire, he backed into the cart, knocking the entire contents into the water. The splash startled the last of the swans still in the water up into the air. Large wings flapped at Peter's head as the startled birds tried to escape, flying directly over Colin.

Colin looked from the swans, to the large white, wet splat of swan sauce that had dropped onto the shoulder of his jacket, to the popcorn still left on the lawn, then up to my balcony. Straight at me. I slid to my knees and watched through the rails.

He pulled off his jacket and shooed the last of the swans back into the water. "Get that cart out," Colin told Peter.

Within a minute, Colin opened the balcony door wide enough for me to fall backward through it.

"So," he said, "What happened this time?"

"I was outside and the door locked so I tried to get Peter's attention." I rolled over and stood up to pretend I was okay.

"Didn't you hear the alarm warning it was about to lock?" he asked in a definite "are you kidding me?" tone.

"Is that what the clicking was? How was I supposed to know that?"

Colin pointed to a sign next to the door. 'Door will click before locking.' You could have called me."

"You had the camera crew with you," I rambled trying to appear less of an idiot than I was. "I didn't want to cause a scene. I know Peter was coming over later so I hoped to get his attention and toss him my key."

"You're dating Peter?" his smile gone.

157

That was a look I'd expect to see from Michael. It was not good. I squirmed. "It's not like that. He's a friend. I'm more like an older sister or something."

"You're not his sister. Not by a long shot." He moved closer, his face dark, unreadable. "You've got something that makes a man feel strong, protective. Don't underestimate what a desirable woman you are."

All moisture in my tongue and lips evaporated. I managed to scratch out "Me?"

"I don't want to see anyone get hurt," he stepped back to the door, like he was afraid of what he might catch from me. "You've been through a lot in two days. Give yourself time to discover what you want. Goodnight Mini."

I spoke to the closed door. "What I want? I can't figure that guy out. Or myself." I pulled my hair back with the headband and looked at my phone. Seven missed calls. I pressed my voice mail button stealing myself for his harsh words, when the screen went black. Dead battery.

"Crap!" It was all the photos from Small World. I could call Michael from the room phone. But he'd see the strange number and I wouldn't be able to keep my secret. One of my options had disappeared.

I slumped onto the side of the bed and studied the phone.

There comes a time when you reach a level of trouble where nothing else matters—like when you stayed out too late as a teenager and you knew you were in big trouble, so you broke another rule on the way home. One more mistake didn't matter.

My secret was shot. Michael would know everything soon. What difference would avoiding his call make? None.

A bizarreness enveloped me as the last tension in my shoulders released and my breathing slowed. Peace. *I think. Insanity, likely.*

Tomorrow I would have to face the part of my life that included an unfaithful husband and my Disney cover up. Tonight I wouldn't have to worry about any other actions. Trouble was trouble. Tonight was mine.

Chapter 23

Peter's tight ass rocked the Prince Charming tights and his shoulders in a gardener's uniform topped the hunk scale. But seeing him in civilian clothes made me want to run upstairs, change into a new outfit, a new hairstyle and a new person.

His pants slid low enough on his hips to be interesting without advertising recent prison release and the light blue shirt he wore matched the exact color of his eyes. Although it was the two tiny orbs accenting his bold pecks that caught my attention.

"Hey Min, you won't believe what happened to me." Peter took my hand and pulled me off at a brisk pace. "Tonight for no reason the swans climbed up on the bank and started pecking at me. I've been working the area all summer and I don't get why they went berserk tonight!"

"I have no idea." One man knowing what an idiot I am was enough.

The first time I'd walked with a man across the park tonight, I was a woman with a secret and a plan to return to my life, unnoticed. Now, whether or not I told Michael's secret, he would soon know mine. He would be back in control.

"Where to?" I asked. I may be too old and too plain to be of interest to Peter, but that didn't stop me from wanting to enjoy him. I held tight to my fantasy.

"I know where to go." He held my hand and we picked up snacks before walking to the dock of the ship. Just like a brother who doesn't want his sister to get lost in a crowd.

His arm touched the small of my back as we walked up the gangplank to the large, white paddle-boat. *I'm sure he's only trying to keep me from falling into the water.*

"I've always loved this old boat," his arm moved to my shoulder as we leaned against the railing. "I've spent many hours at night circling the park memorizing my auditions lines. I've always worked well with white noise. Some people might think I'm a little touched. Then I explain I'm an actor studying for a part. Usually I can find someone who'll read with me."

Probably a young and cute someone. "That must be helpful..."

"People always love to help actors. There's a lot of ham inside all of us, I guess. It's helpful to hear how my own voice bounces off my environment."

"I know what you mean. I remember studying my lines and the other world I would go into. The same thing helped when I was working on nursing. I'd be memorizing the muscles and bones of the body, but no one wanted to help then."

"It's hard for me to believe you'd leave your talents to go into nursing." He moved closer until we stood against the rail, watching the tied up boats bob against the dock at Tom Sawyers Island. I gazed up in time to catch his glance down my blouse.

"It seemed like the right idea at the time," I grabbed my top from the back and tugged a bit to spoil Peter's view. "It was my husband's idea, but if I had been completely fulfilled, I never would have changed."

"I've never switched, never faltered. I've always known exactly which direction I wanted to go in then I take off like a rocket. I only need my first break." His arm had begun rubbing up and down the small of my back. "If you were meant to be in the theater no one could have changed your mind."

"I suppose that's true," I squeaked as his hand dropped to my hip. "You do realize I'm several years older than you."

"I'm an actor, I adapt. Besides you could pass for my age." I pretended that was a rational answer.

I bit off the end of a chocolate, caramel-covered marshmallow I'd found in my pocket and I dug around looking for something to say. Hopefully the stickiness would keep my mouth from hanging open.

"I find that older women have a lot more to offer." His hand slipped down and brushed my butt, enhanced by hours of yard work and two days of chocolate-dipped Disney.

"Well look at those lights," I blurted as we passed the entrance to New Orleans Square again and came to dock. I was too old for a young man-boy who collected older woman as love professors. I don't have anything I could teach him. Michael was my only lover, although I'd never called him that before.

"Let's go around again," he said. I waited to see the humor and playfulness in his eyes but those beautiful blue orbs were sultry and serious. *Escape!*

"Or we could go on Thunder Mountain," I said as I tried to diffuse the tension in my brain—the fight between throwing myself at him and throwing myself overboard. The boat was too private, too personal. "I've never been on it."

"The last row of the train gives you the best rush," he said. I'd absorbed exactly enough flattery and sugar that crack-the-whip at the end of a roller coaster sounded fun.

I cased the ride, no large drops, plunges or other despicable surprises played upon park guests. A miniature train engine pulled a dozen carts around a mountain. We boarded the last car and clacked our way upward through the decorated southwestern buttes and skulls that reminded me of Mother Gunderson's Lancaster living room.

Anticipating terror we whipped down our first corner with no sudden drops. It was a turbulent ride where gravity and hormones pushed me against Peter.

Laughing out in relief that the ride held none of the Splash Mountain sudden drops, I didn't want to get out at the end of the ride. Peter flashed my badge to the loader – brushing his hand against my breast. I doubted it was an accident.

The freedom of flying through the ride, combined with the physical touch of a good looking guy, was the release I wasn't even aware I had been looking for until it happened. When Peter took my hand at the end of the ride I didn't pull it back like a married woman.

"What's next?" Peter asked.

"Jungle Cruise?" I wanted to race around the park and gobble up every sensation.

On the brisk walk through Frontierland to Adventureland, I watched every woman under thirty five ogle Peter. And every female employee called him by name. He nodded to them all and talked about his life, school, musicals and a commercial he'd been in.

Everything about his life was alive. I started to talk about how Dad loved to tease me about the hippopotamus on the Jungle Cruise, but Amber, the boat driver interrupted, talking to Peter like they were old friends and maybe more.

Watching Peter volley jokes with Amber amused the visitors. I hoped everyone couldn't see my lustful doe eyes as easily as Amber's.

I kept my vision averted. From the totem pole scene deep in the Amazon to the waterfall, I thought of all the traveling I wished I'd done. Peter had spent last summer in Europe and planned to move to New York at the end of the semester. I tried to take Colin's warning seriously when Peter held my hand during the ride, but it was too obscure to believe.

He bought me meat on a stick and we climbed the rope ladders that circled the large tree of Tarzan's tree house. I missed the Swiss Family Robinson version.

"Everyone likes you here," I said. *Especially me.* "You're such a natural. Why not stay and work here? A career at Disneyland?"

"I've been asked, but I need to follow my dreams," he pulled me to the entrance of the Indiana Jones ride and I was ready to follow his dreams too. Nothing could scare me tonight, except maybe him. We sat in the front row of the huge jeep which carried us through the center choice of three doors.

An animatronics version of Harrison Ford at the start took my mind off Peter for a moment as the jeep weaved and jolted through scenes with all Jones' nemesis: snakes, rats and spiders. Our legs bumped together through the dark ride.

We didn't say a word on our walk back through the park, and I fought the urge to grab his tight butt. Probably a result of being off birth control pills for the past weeks—combined with Michael's adultery and my desire to procreate. I was in heat.

The high Fantasyland clock was almost at four in the morning by the time we'd reached my door. I slid the key through the pad then grabbed the knob. Peter touched my shoulders, turned me and kissed me. The one sign of time passing was the growing cramp in my hand where I still held the knob.

If he hadn't been wearing my Mango Minnie lipstick I wouldn't have believed it happened. I was so shocked I didn't realize I was being kissed. *What a shame. I missed everything.*

What the hell! Nothing here is real anyway. I leaned forward, took his wide shoulders in my hands and pulled him in for a kiss of my own.

"Goodnight." I croaked, still tingling from my first kiss with a prince. I slunk up the stairs and into bed. I should have said goodbye. My fairy tale was ending.

Chapter 24

A persistent knocking pulled my eyes open in the morning light. I was tempted to cover my head with a pillow and fall back into my dream replaying Peter's kiss until I smelled breakfast.

I threw back the covers to stand up, but was tangled in my nightgown—green, filmy and long. I was more tired last night than I'd thought. I didn't remember putting this on. I stood and reached a foot out for the comfort of my Donald Duck feet slippers but instead found a pair of high-heeled kitten slippers with fuzzy tops and decorated with a tiny pink shell.

Clipping across the floor dragging a green train, I was ready to show Felicity that I was game to try anything.

I opened the door to a mermaid.

Ariel stood pushing a tray of food, wearing her white wedding gown and golden crown. Her thick, red hair cascading down her back looked real.

"Hello," I curtsied, though not quite sure why. "That's a pretty fancy costume for delivering food."

"I want to welcome all our guests." She pushed the tray to the table's edge and began unloading and uncovering platters of hot meats, fruits and rolls. "I hope you slept well."

"Oh, so you're a hostess like Felicity," I tripped backward on the long gown I wore and caught my balance on the desk.

"I'm Ariel," she set out a coffee service. *"I'm marrying Eric today and I want all the wedding guests to be comfortable."*

"Oh, I get it. You're staying in role." The food under the metal lids smelled lovely. *"Won't you join me?"*

"Just for coffee," she sat at the table, motioning for me to join her. *"I'm having brunch with my father, King Triton, back home before the ceremony."*

I pulled the back length of my nightgown up and tried to look confident wearing elegant negligees. If she planned to stay in character, I'd play along. *"So you don't always stay on dry land?"*

"I will most of the time with Eric. Though I do miss the water so I'm lucky. I can still go back and visit my family."

"The best of both worlds?" I watched her pour the hot coffee into both cups, then without asking she added the exact amount of milk I would have added. You have to love the attention to detail at the park.

"Exactly. I wasn't meant to live in only one world." She checked the mirror beside her and fussed with her already perfect tresses. I couldn't tell where her real hair ended and the wig must begin.

I envied her. Or at least the part she played. She knew what she wanted, went after it and won it all. That would be the real Key to the Castle for someone who didn't even know where to start. *"I know what you mean, but I'm not sure which world is for me."*

168

"You know," Ariel leaned over the desk and placed a hand on my shoulder, "my father tried to nail my fins to the floor, but sometimes you have to be free. Decide what you want, then fight for it."

"He sounds like my dad," I stirred the coffee with a tiny silver spoon, enjoying the tinkle as it hit the ceramic sides. "He tried to get me to make up my mind. Decide what I wanted, then go for it. Not to let anyone stand in my way."

My throat constricted. I hadn't thought of Dad or Mom all day yesterday. I couldn't remember the last time they weren't in my thoughts.

"My father wanted me to stay under the sea and always be his little girl." Ariel said and stabbed a piece of star fruit and took a small bite, careful not to drop it on her gown. "I had to ruin both of his dreams for me."

"Dad would be disappointed to see me now," I slumped back in the chair.

"How can that be?" Ariel asked. "If you had a father who only wanted whatever you wanted, how is it possible for him to ever be unhappy with you?"

A few tears spilled out along with the words. I was so desperate, baring my soul to a stranger.

"Because I don't know what I want," I cried and threw my hands up. My knuckles hit the tall crystal orange juice carafe and knocked it onto Ariel's white dress.

I sprung up and found myself propped on a pile of gold satin pillows in a pink sleep shirt dotted with mice prints.

What would Freud say about dreams that included breakfast with mermaids?

Chapter 25

Reality was hard to see past the soft blue gossamer bed drapes that shaded the late morning light. The memory of Michael kissing Jessica no longer cut off my breathing. Not in the hours since I had kissed a prince.

I squeezed a lace-covered pillow to my chest and searched for a memory of the last time Michael's lips had curled my toes.

Guilt nagged at me after I realized a lack of guilt. I blamed myself for not blaming myself.

The cell phone lay dead on the nightstand. I slipped past into the bathroom for a long soak in equal parts hot water, bubbles and denial.

My fingertips ripened into raisins as I popped the clear orbs as if pulling petals off a daisy. About three hundred 'he loves me' to two hundred and ninety nine 'he loves me not.' I quit while I was ahead and before I could force myself to ask who 'he' was.

Waving my arm across the remaining suds, I searched for a way back to my marriage. Had we both gone too far? Even though I'd kept my clothes on so far. There was no simple answer, if I even had a choice.

I could leave Michael. I wouldn't be homeless. At least not at first. Michael would surely take me to court over the house. To get his half he wouldn't care if I had to live in a car. Except I didn't own a car.

171

At least I had the beginnings of new friends. Although since I'd met them yesterday, it was probably too soon in our relationship to ask to move in.

We could try to repair the damage with counseling— to find our way back to whatever it was that drew us together. That would take tremendous desire and may not even work.

I had no answers, but I understood most of the questions. The most important would be the one both Dad and Ariel would have asked. *What do I want?*

To do anything, I had to take the first step. I needed a direction.

Slipping into the thick terry armor of my Disneyland bathrobe I steeled myself for the call that had to be made from the bedside Mickey Mouse phone, since my cell had died an early death.

Michael knows I'm not at home. I have never missed his calls. He would have tried the house phone after I didn't pick up the cell. What would he have done after that?

What would I do if I couldn't get a hold of him all night? I'd have been worried sick. I would have called the police. I couldn't picture Michael pacing, but I could see him worrying that his lawn wasn't done. He'd call in the Cavalry for that.

Quick and easy was my plan. I'd leave a message for him at work. His cell phone would be notified he had a message. He could check it from Vegas and I'd be off the hook.

I'd admit where I was, then hang up and go on with my last day.

"Hello," Michael's voice was strong.

"Uh, it's Mini—Margaret! Margaret. It's Margaret." I blurted at a speed previously reserved for attempts to explain the harm done to course grass by un-stomped divots prior to Michael's eyes glazing over.

"You've reached Michael Gunderson," his voice continued. *Voicemail!* "Please leave a message and I'll return it as soon as I land."

The pause after his recorded greeting tied my tongue in a knot. I stood up, held the phone away from my face and blurted to get the message out before the machine stopped.

"I'm still at Disneyland. I won a prize that includes lodging. I'll be home after the four-thirty parade is over. I'm Queen."

I slammed down the phone as if it was too hot to hold, then stared as if I expected it to say something. It rang within twenty seconds. I threw a pillow at it and ran into the bathroom.

After fifteen minutes my hair threatened to ignite if I didn't turn off the dryer. Once I hit the switch, the sound of the ringing phone made my heart race like I'd swallowed a wind-up clock. The blinking message light on the Mickey Mouse phone pulsed out 'Call Michael.'

He had probably Googled the prize by now and read about the pass, the travel and all the other perks of my prize which I hadn't even read about yet. And that the travel portion was worth a fortune if I gave it up.

The phone rang twice and sliced through my confidence while I finished with my mascara and slipped into a pair of Tinker Bell panties. But when I opened the armoire to the wardrobe Felicity selected and spied a new top, the fear vanished.

173

Lime green and covered in multi-colored balloons, the shirt read "It's my Birthday!"

I'd forgotten the day I'd been looking forward to for so long.

"This may be my last day here for a long while so I need to make it the best ever," I told the room. No response—a good omen.

I couldn't draw any more attention to the girls if they were glowing neon, but I didn't care. If I believed Peter's stares, my breasts were my best asset.

Plus there'd be time enough to change back into my own drab clothes after the parade.

I snuck up on the ringing phone, hung up the call and put the receiver under the pillow. I grabbed my bag and ran for the door. The familiar weight hit my shoulder heavier than usual so I locked the purse inside and hurried away carrying only the Key to the Castle.

Chapter 26

Like two animated buzzards sitting on a fence, one side of my brain asked "What do you want to do?" while the other side replied, "I don't know; what do you want to do?"

I ran to the statue of Walt Disney and collapsed on a wooden bench facing the length of Main Street. I'd made it out of the room and past the point of having to talk to Michael until tonight.

The park was full of people and noisy with activity—laughter, cries and the roar of the rides. The sounds helped slow my rapid heartbeat and I let the park sink in. Surrounded by banks of rainbow-colored flower beds at the hub of the park, I had a view of Frontierland on my right and Tomorrowland on the left.

Instead of worrying about my crumbled life, I focused on what to eat for breakfast and how to spend my last day at the park.

The smell of the corn dog cart at the end of Main Street called to me the same way I'm sure it always did to Dad. But I held out, forcing myself to take everything in before diving forward.

Ahead on the opposite side of the street I spotted the pink and white-striped awning of the Carnation Café and Bakery.

Once all my senses were tuned into the present—and the park—I set off for the Café. I paused to let a horse-drawn wagon pass when I heard my name.

Felicity waved and hurried over.

"Happy Birthday, Mini," Felicity caught up with me, not even out of breath, her daily park exercise keeping her round shape quick and agile. "I thought you'd be sleeping in today. You had a pretty late night."

"Uh," *Oops, does she know I'd kissed a prince? Change the subject!* "I had the weirdest dream. The Little Mermaid brought me breakfast. It was so real, I had to get up and eat."

"Right," Felicity smiled. She so knew I was with Peter. Was I a fallen woman? "So where did you pick to eat?"

"Carnation," I pointed, relieved that we were talking about food versus whether or not I was a slut. "I love the little courtyard."

"Would you like some company or did you want to people watch alone?"

"Definitely company." Being around people the last few days reminded me that I am not the hermit I'd been pretending to be for the last few years.

We were shown to a table closest to the sidewalk which allowed the greatest viewing options. We waited for our order, then conspired on what the different people must be thinking, if they were having fun or if they needed to give a child a nap.

"We should have a sign on the front gate to warn women not to wear high-heeled shoes to Disneyland," Felicity nodded toward a twenty-something girl in a short skirt and stilettos. "They may be smiling on the way in all dressed up wedding style, but they will be crying like a funeral on the way out."

I tried not to think of Jessica's shoes. She hadn't stayed at the park long enough for her feet to hurt. Steaming plates of food were set in front of us and I busied myself filling each square nook of my waffle with butter before dousing with syrup.

"So how's it going for you Mini?" Felicity stirred the whipped cream into her cocoa. "Have you enjoyed your prize so far?"

"Oh yes. It's just that life has gotten in the way a bit." That was the most polite way I could describe what had been happening. I stabbed several small pieces of strawberry until my fork was loaded. "This has been a dream. Today I want a few more hours where I try hard to enjoy the present. The end of the day will come soon enough."

"That sounds dire," Felicity touched my hand and the pull to cuddle on her shoulder and let her solve all my problems was fierce. I thought back to my first problem solvers.

"Don't worry if you don't have a roomful of friends," Dad had said when we'd waited for the first person to arrive at my seventh birthday party, twenty minutes after the My Little Pony invitations read it was to begin. "Through your entire life, you only need one."

I'd been shy about delivering the invitations at school, so Mom had dropped them in the mailboxes of all the little girls who lived on our street.

When no one showed up that afternoon, Mom blamed it on summer vacation, packed me into the car and by three o'clock we were at Disneyland and I was holding Mickey's hand. I did have friends. They lived close, though I only saw them once a year.

"You know there's nothing you can't do if you break it down and tackle it piece by piece," Felicity's voice brought me back to the present.

"My list is pretty long." I sipped at my pulpy orange juice and waited for it to join the sugary syrup and raise my energy level.

"Try me."

"I have to cash in the Key to the Castle." I pulled the truth out with a speed hoping that would reduce the pain. It didn't. "Or at least the travel portion."

"Oh dear," Felicity pushed her unfinished plate to the side and leaned forward. "Are you sure? I thought you would be the perfect one to truly appreciate this gift."

"I am," my voice cracked. "But if Michael and I managed to make a go of it, I wouldn't be able to travel around the world while he was at home. And he would never want to go. If it doesn't work out for us, then I'd need the money from the prize to buy back the other half of my parent's house."

"Of course it's up to you," Felicity said. "I'd love for you to be able to enjoy the full prize. You're exactly the type of fan I hoped would win—traveling all over the world, representing Disneyland as the Happiest Place on Earth. But I'm happy it will offer you some financial security."

She was so nice, letting me off easy. I wish that had made me feel better, instead of exposing a raw sense of loss.

"If you want," I said, leaving my meal unfinished, "we can go back to the Castle and I'll sign the papers."

"There's no hurry. Once you sign though, it is final." Felicity stood up. "We can take care of that after the parade. I have to go. I'll check in with you later. What are you going to do?"

"I don't know. Even with as many times I've been here," I waved to the park, "places and attractions I've never seen. I don't even know which ride to go on next."

"These might help," Felicity brushed the crumbs off her skirt and pulled a park map and pen out of her pocket. "Now I'll leave you to your day until it's time to get ready for the parade. If I miss you, have anyone from guest services call me and I'll escort you back to change."

The table was cleared so I ordered a chocolate éclair for breakfast dessert and unfolded the map.

I began checking off each ride, store and attraction I'd completed in the last two days. That left a smatter of holes in Critter Country, Adventureland, New Orleans Square and Frontierland. Tomorrowland and Toon Town were untouched.

I tipped the water-filled cylinder back and forth and watched a small encased crab swim end to end in the liquid. Everything reminded me of The Little Mermaid this morning. She braved it all for what she wanted.

Quitting had gotten me into my position, stripped me of options, and would probably cause me to lose the biggest prize in Disneyland's history.

That was when I knew. For the first time, I would finish something—go on or into every ride, store and attraction in Disneyland before I left today.

Tami Casias

Chapter 27

Zigzagging between camera shopping, posing for a hand-cut silhouette, listening to Abe Lincoln's Gettysberg address and strolling past early park models, I'd finished Main Street. I treated myself like royalty and sent my loot back to the Castle and boarded the train. If this would be my last visit for a while, I wanted to remember every detail.

I hopped off at New Orleans Square to visit the Christmas store. *I do love to shop.*

I didn't realize the level of my rebellion until I had purchased eighty-two ornaments. I wasn't exactly sure what I would do with them since Michael didn't celebrate Christmas.

Holidays were hooey for Michael. A lot of work for nothing. And his parents agreed. Since I was without family, I had to adjust to the Gunderson way. *I could change that—celebrate holidays and birthdays. Display family pictures on the mantle.*

I didn't want my old life back. With Michael or without, I wanted a new one.

Worrying about how to bring up the holiday talk with Michael sucked out the bravado that the ornaments had injected. I slipped into the Creole restaurant for mental nourishment.

Spicy jambalaya and chunks of dipping bread surrounded me and soon I was up to my fingers in the juiced-up enjoyment where anything was possible. I wiped the last bits of sauce off my fingers and reached for my map as Colin appeared.

"You're by yourself?" Colin sat on one of the wire chairs. "I'm surprised. I thought you and Peter were an item now."

I took a chug of the iced tea to wash down the last bite of bread and embarrassment. *Did he see me kiss Peter?* I didn't know what to say. I had no experience as a hussy.

"It's a small park when it comes to gossip. I'd be careful if I were you." If he had smiled, or appeared concerned I might have thought he cared. But he was stern. Demanding. "You are married."

Buzz kill. I stood up fast enough to bump the table, rattling the silverware against the plate.

"Look," I pointed a finger at his chest, "I don't have to explain myself to someone who is too afraid to open up to another person. Just because I want a family of my own that I don't have to share with a twenty-two year old. I'm not saying it's Peter. I'm saying I'm leaving the option open that maybe returning to an unhappy existence with a cheating husband might not be my single choice. Thanks for clearing it up. I don't have a choice. That's a great birthday gift."

He had some nerve. I wasn't perfect, but he didn't have to go out of his way to point out my insignificance. I hurried away, struggling not to cry. I wanted to be a grown-up woman, who, when confronted by a disagreeable man could best him with logic and reason.

But I cried. Enough water spilled out of my eyes to make walking blurry. I stopped when the park did at the end of Critter Country. Then, I circled back, boarded the train and melted into a blob on the wooden bench.

I faced away from the platforms, so that at each land when a new group arrived, they wouldn't see my pathetic tears. After three or four times past the dinosaur scene I'd managed to calm down just as I was tapped on the shoulder.

"You're circling," Colin stood next to me.

"My mind wandered I guess," I looked out at edge of Toon Town and ended my train trip. "How'd you know where I was?"

"Every employee at this park seems to know you by name," Colin stood aside and I stepped off the train into the small station. "I made you pretty mad at the restaurant. I wanted to make sure you were all right."

"Shouldn't I be?" I said. "After all, I'm alone. No one wants me."

"I'm sorry," he kicked the wood floor with the toe of one foot. "I had no right to say anything to hurt you. You've been through a lot in a short time. You have the right to be happy. Especially on your birthday."

The anger seeped out of me and I fought to keep the tears from spilling again. "You don't have to say all that. It's okay. I know Peter is way too young and cute for me. My chance for true love and a family are gone. I wanted to pretend a little bit longer."

"I don't believe that," he reached out as if to touch my face, then dropped his hand. "You are an attractive woman. Lots of men will think so. Make sure you're doing what you want for yourself."

"That would be a lot easier if I knew what that was." I turned toward the flower bed to ensure no droplets rolled down my cheeks before I could blink them away.

183

Colin touched my elbow and held out my map.

"You left this. It had a lot of notes so I thought you might want to keep it," he smiled, trying to lighten the mood. "What were you doing before I ruined your morning?"

The crumpled map was tattered on the edges where I'd pulled it in and out of my pocket multiple times, but it couldn't have looked any more beautiful.

"Thank you," I unfolded the map and checked off the train—relieved to focus on something happy. "I'm not known for finishing things. I want to change that, so I'm going to visit every ride, store and attraction at this park before I leave today."

"A birthday mission." Colin rubbed his palms together. "It's okay to say no, but can I play?"

"You've done everything a million times," I said. *Not to mention you were just a big—.*

"And I am a jerk." he finished for me. My poker face sucks. The more I tried to keep from nodding in agreement, the more twisted up my mouth became. "Your face says it all. Let me make it up to you? Give me another chance?"

"Okay," I couldn't stay mad at someone who loved the park as much as I did. I pointed to the map. "I've finished these lands, but I still have everything with a circle."

"Then let's get going," he pulled the receiver out of his ear and slipped it into his pocket, turned off the radio and waved me forward to the entrance of Toon Town.

At the massive gates I stared ahead into the land that looked like an animation cell.

Up the slight grade past a huge bank of parked strollers, we landed at Roger Rabbit's Cartoon Spin. "You'll love this one," Colin opened the exit gate and I followed him into the front past a long line of visitors. "When you have more time you should go through the queue. There are some great scenes."

Colin slid into a puffy and tiny yellow New York City taxi cab. I was still disturbed by his reaction to Peter, but by the time we laughed through the bright fluorescent path, and through a rabbit hole at the end, the tension eased.

We grabbed a hot dog and walked through Minnie's miniature house—homage to pink—from the settee to the rugs to the washing machine.

"Tell the truth," Colin asked as I stood in front of the oven watching a frosted cake rise through the glass. "This would be your ideal kitchen."

I pushed the button on the blender and watched it swirl. "Well, it's close. I do think a few other colors would be great too, though. This is a feminine house."

"Wait until you see Mickey's."

We walked past a wishing well and I touched my ringless finger. I looked up at Colin who stared straight at me.

"Let's go!" I hurried past the vegetable garden and up the front steps. Mickey's was a man's mouse. The living room was filled with sporting items, a television and a recliner. A trip through his garden shed ended in a barn with a showing of his early cartoons.

Colin followed me through, taking me in as I took in the scenery. "Do you have to keep staring at me?"

"I'm sorry!" Colin smiled. "It's so much fun to be with someone experiencing the park for the first time."

185

The exit shuffled guests through a special room one at a time where they could have their picture taken with Mickey. I waved Colin over to us. "Come on. We're on this adventure together!"

Once outside, I climbed through Chip and Dale's Treehouse on my own. Colin said he was too big and spent the time on the phone. I imagined him stuck in the small opening of the slide. By the time I'd figured my way out, he had finished his call and his jacket and tie had disappeared.

"Getting comfy?" I asked.

"I wasn't dressed to play," he said.

We rode the tiny Gadgets Go Coaster that actually pumped more adrenaline that it appeared it would, then explored Donald's Sailing Boat. When I slipped off my shoes to jump in Goofy's Playhouse I expected Colin to wait outside.

"I wouldn't miss this one," he said, and made sure we had a few moments of jumping on the net-circled air mattress without any small children inside to squish. He bounced with calculation, landing close enough to my feet to shoot me up in the air. He made a great show out of one bounce and I flew up into him, knocking him onto his back and me on top.

"Uh!" The air slammed out of both of us and I missed hitting his face with mine by a nose.

"Are you all right?" he asked, his breath warm and caramel scented.

"I think so," I laughed, taking a mental count of unbroken ribs. Colin slid his hands up my sides which stopped sound and time. My lips wondered if I was in a frenzy of kissing new men when he lifted me up and rolled me off.

"And that's why we don't rough house," the young woman at the gate told the next batch of children ready to play. "Someone always gets hurt."

Stifling my smile and confusion, I slid out to put my shoes on. I watched Colin retie his wingtips while I tried to figure out how to get past the awkward silence and ask Colin to join me for lunch.

"Ready to eat?" he asked, offering me a hand to stand up.

His hands were exceptionally large, but somehow mine fit. "Are you reading my mind?"

"No, but I can hear your stomach growling."

I shoved him at the shoulder and laughed. "I'd pretend to be embarrassed, but I'm sure you could. Where should we go?"

"I've planned a little surprise for you. Are you game?"

"Are you kidding? I'm at Disneyland. Of course I'm game."

Colin led me past the gates and we veered to the right through a large crowd standing in the back to see the Princess Fantasy Fair. He held out his hand to me so he wouldn't lose me in the crowd. His grip was strong and warm. We weaved to the front side where he had a table set up for me with a large picnic basket.

"You are going all out for the prize winner," I said. "If you weren't already the boss, I'd send a recommendation letter for you."

Colin held out my chair. "This isn't part of the prize. This is how I treat a fellow Disney addict."

"Thanks, but I prefer fanatic." I crossed off all the rides in Toon Town. Each cross was an earned merit badge.

Chapter 28

Giant dolls danced out of the Small World clock announcing the passing of another hour. Reality chased me toward the Canal Boats.

Colin sat next to me and rolled up the sleeves on his dress shirt. "Whew, it's getting warmer. I'm not dressed for a race."

I pointed to a shop next to the Tea Cup ride as we turned the corner into Monstro's Mouth. "Why don't you grab a t-shirt? That is, if you're in it for the full ride?" I hoped he'd say yes.

"I've cancelled everything else until the parade."

I smiled behind my camera and took photos of the miniature houses and Bonsai trees.

"Here," he took the camera, "let me take one of you."

"I'll take one of both of you," A woman across from me offered.

Colin and I looked at each other for a second and shrugged "okay." I was creating quite a scrapbook page that I could never show anyone else.

He draped an arm over my shoulder and I was glad he couldn't see the smile I had on. I had another friend. And I was counting.

On the way to Frontierland we made what I thought would be a quick detour into a store for Colin to buy a t-shirt. But he hemmed and hawed longer than I do when forced to shop.

"What are you? A girl?" I asked. "I thought guys were decisive."

"This is important," Colin said, holding up a choice of two shirts—a brown Peter Pan battling Captain Hook and a black shirt with white skull and logo from 'The Nightmare Before Christmas.' "I'm trying to remember if I already have this one."

I grabbed the black one and put it back on the rack. "I'm on the clock. Get the brown one. I'm not a fan of wearing skulls on the outside."

He handed me his shirt to hold and I tried not to be one of the several women in the store staring at the ripples his chest muscles made as he raised his arms to pull the shirt over his head. But my eyes were glued. That chest had held me up numerous times in the past two days. This was the first time I'd been able to see the strength—not to mention the small patch of black curling hair that stretched between each nipple. While he filled out a tag to send his shirt to package pickup, I listened to the girl at the register flirt with the park boss.

I hoped I didn't sound that obvious. Here I'd found a man that was exactly what I wanted—good looking, sexy and a big fan of games. The two problems were that I was married and he wasn't interested in me.

Logic—an unfamiliar acquaintance—told me that I was looking for a man to want me because my husband hadn't. *Screw logic.*

If this were my first day at the park, I would have walked from one attraction to another, not missing an inch between. But with the deadline hanging over me, we ran haphazard from spot to missing spot, crossing out the holes on the map to complete a full park visit. Then we circled.

The first time around Tom Sawyer's Island on the Rivers of America we paddled Davy Crockett Canoes, then went around again aboard the Columbia Sailing ship. Neither of us mentioned the Riverboat. He must have known I'd ridden that with Peter last night. He knew everything that happened at Disneyland.

I'd already been to all of Main Street, but still we rode back and forth on the Omnibus, the streetcar, and then in the Clydesdales' wagon. The best part up to then had been strapping into a log on the Matterhorn. I snuggled against Colin's chest as the log rattled and jerked through the lair of the Abominable Snowman's territory.

Still vibrating from the ride and a bit of desire, I checked off the last attraction in seven of the eight park lands.

"Only Tomorrowland left," I sighed.

"Was that a happy or sad sigh?" Colin asked.

"Both. I'm excited about all the new rides but I've been on Space Mountain before and it scared the crap out of me and was nauseating."

Colin grabbed both my shoulders and leaned down, eye to eye. "I believe you can do it. You've mastered the other mountain."

"I wouldn't call screaming my way through the ride as mastered," I smiled. "More like I survived."

"Then save it for last."

Four rides and two shows later I took a break at a multi-colored table under a pepper tree next to

Innoventions and spread out my map. I spied a food cart I hadn't tried yet—chocolate or popcorn next?

"Salty or sweet?" Colin's deep voice interrupted my internal snack debate. "Although I can't figure out where you put all the food you eat."

I thought I caught him taking a quick look at my chest, perhaps confirming the spelling on my shirt. He walked to the stand and brought back a large popcorn and two sodas.

"What's left?" Colin sat across from me and turned the map, his large hand taking in the rides without the x's while I took in the lines of his shoulders under the new Disney shirt.

"Pretty much everything on this end," I waved to my right, "and Autopia and Buzz Lightyear. Where do we start?"

"Anywhere you want," he said.

"Buzz Lightyear? That's new for me."

Colin smiled and held out the box so I could grab a handful of popcorn. "I do like that one."

"Have you been on it much?"

Colin reached into the box and pulled out half the popcorn in one scoop. "Enough."

We dashed through the florescent arcade game. I shot at the targets. Colin hit them, every one. He pulverized my score, proving all the lunch hours he killed on this ride were well spent.

Next we went to Autopia, where I insisted on driving.

"My dad gave me my first driving lessons in these cars," I reminisced as Colin folded his long legs into the red convertible.

"My father didn't believe in automobiles," Colin laughed. "They cause pollution and keep people in too big of a hurry. He was an original hippie out of Dublin, Ireland. He came to America with my mom before I was born, to sing and dance in a band of renaissance players."

"How can you live without a car?" I needed to know since I may be without access to a car soon.

"They live in San Francisco on the Muni line so they don't need one."

I slowed to avoid bumping the car in front of us. "So how do your folks feel about your career? Disneyland is definitely not low-tech."

"He supports all of my choices. Whatever I believe in, whatever makes me happy, makes him happy."

"That sounds like my dad."

"Hey Princess Mini," Dad called from a car behind me on my eighth or ninth birthday, "slow down."

I raced with the pedal down as far as it would go in the hopes that the train of silver-sequin-edged chiffon attached to the point of my pink princess hat would wave in the breeze.

I turned to see him trying to catch up with me, but his car had other plans. "Race you to the finish line," I'd called.

The road climbed up a ramp to cross the traffic going the other way.

"What are you thinking?" Colin asked.

"I'm a good driver, paying attention to the road," I was over painting the roses red. It was so much better to remember the happy times with my parents than to beat myself up about mistakes I'd made along the way. And

I saw the finish line—for the first time I would complete something.

"You have the same look on your face as you did when you tasted the first kernel of hot popcorn."

"Happy memories, that's all," I patted the side of the car before climbing out.

"Your parents weren't hippies, then?" Colin asked as we walked over to the House of Innoventions.

"No, fairly conservative. They did want me to have everything I wanted though. It hurt them when I chose something they knew was going to hurt me." *Like marrying Michael.*

"I bet they'd still be happy for you, if you were happy too."

"I think about them all the time," I said. "Their happy marriage looked so easy from the outside."

My feet were starting to throb when we sat down again in the kitchen of the future demo. I played with a built-in flat screen on the counter with daily menu planning ideas, while Colin worked with a refrigerator that added items to a virtual grocery list when they were removed from the shelf.

I tried to envision his home. "Is your house full of high-tech?" I asked.

"I have to admit it's similar to my office, plus tons of photos from my nieces and nephews," he said. "I like old comfortable furniture, but appreciate modern too. I'm still waiting for my flying car."

"I know what you mean," I played with the computer. "I'd like an overstuffed chair and one of those old wooden tables that are so scratched that they look perfect. But I do admire a good TV."

"It's hard to find someone who likes the best of the old and still open to the new." Colin was so close I fought the urge to grab my second kissing victim. "I wonder what the future will look like."

I leaned forward a little. He leaned forward a little. Our mutual lean was about to end in a kiss. My hands slid over the computer buttons on the counter and a hidden television popped up between us and grazed my chin.

"I guess it's time to go back to the present," Colin waved me forward.

My overactive imagination, stimulated by recent trauma and a royal kiss, must have seen something that wasn't there. Outside I pulled the map from my pocket and crossed off the last couple of rides.

"What's left?" Colin asked.

"You know..." I looked toward Space Mountain. My heart raced.

Colin walked a few steps, then turned to me shaking his head. "You don't have to go. There's no harm in choosing not to do something that you know you won't enjoy."

"I'm tempted," I looked at the sloped roof of the ride, topped with a slender spire, and resisted the urge to crawl into the safety of his arms. "But I need to finish."

"How about some caloric courage?" he waved to the food carts near us.

"Surprise me." Again. The first surprise was how easy he was to be around. I watched him walk toward the vendors and wished my husband was fun to be with.

A pair of arms grabbed me from behind and then lifted and swung me around, flinging my thoughts out of my head and the map to the ground. I was too startled to scream.

"Mini, I have great news," Peter said. "I got a gig in New York. It's off-off Broadway, but it's an existing show so I've got a three-month commitment," Peter cried. "And you won't believe how it happened. An assistant of someone who I auditioned for last week was in the Golden Horseshoe Review and heard me sing. That's what did it! You are totally my lucky charm."

"Great Peter! You're going to do well. I'm sure I'll hear you're famous someday soon." I spin around twice seeing Colin's face both times staring at me holding two chocolate dipped rice treats in his hands.

"Hmmm," Colin cleared his throat and handed me a snack, then stood between Peter and I. "We were in the middle of something Peter."

I bit through the chewy goodness and watched the Peter and Colin show. Colin was the only one playing.

"What are you doing?" Peter asked.

I swallowed the bite, rubbing chocolate off my teeth with my tongue before answering. "I want to go on every ride here and I only have one left," I pointed to Space Mountain.

"Cool—that's one of my favorites," Peter grabbed my free hand and pulled me to the gate. He was completely and beautifully clueless to the look he received from Colin. I wasn't sure how to describe it myself.

"But Colin was going to," I started.

"Do what you want," Colin tossed his untasted treat into a waste can. "I have work to get back to."

My safety net and new friend left me with Peter.

Chapter 29

Space Mountain stared back at my nervous eyes. I didn't want my fears to let Disneyland become one more thing I'd leave undone. But still I hesitated. *I'd almost rather see Michael right now.*

"You're shaking," Peter nuzzled my neck, his cheeks smooth and soft. "We don't have to do this if you don't want to. I couldn't wait to talk to you about something anyway. My friend is putting me up rent free as long as I want. As long as you want, if you come with me."

"What?" *I must be hallucinating from a pre-ride panic.* "But we just met!" *What a ridiculous thing to say. How about you're younger, prettier and I'm married.*

"I know it's crazy," Peter said, "but that's what makes it great. After knowing each other a couple of days you've already gotten me the best job I've ever had. You totally get why this is so important to me and you need a place to go anyway."

"I do?"

"Aren't you leaving that guy who cheated on you?" Peter pulled me closer to the ride's fast-pass line. So matter of fact—an obvious answer.

What was not obvious were the details. How would I actually leave? How could I keep the legacy my parents wanted for me?

"I don't know," I said. "I mean, there's so much to consider." *Whether my racing heart would explode due to Space Mountain anxiety, the thought of giving up the Key to the Castle in a couple of hours, how many gym hours I'd have to accomplish before the possibility of Peter seeing me without clothes on….*

"Don't worry, you can sleep on the couch," Peter ran a finger down the side of my face. "I'm pretty superstitious. I want my good luck charm near me. We can practice my lines together and you can take all the time you want to figure out what you want to do. Let's go to your room and talk this out. Our future."

My mouth opened and I lifted one finger up to him. "One second," I said, then bolted through the closest escape route into Space Mountain.

Peter laughed and ran behind me, then slipped ahead into the rocket, patting the seat for me.

Ridiculous. Wrong. A joke. I opened my mouth to laugh off his odd sense of humor, but one look into his naïve, sexy, trusting eyes and I was shocked to see he wasn't kidding. That was when I drooled. Could I run away? Go and not face Michael or anything?

We were seated in the front of the rocket-shaped car and a safety bar came over my neck locking me into position. A bad sign. No other ride had required more than safety strap or lap bar.

Of all the sounds at Disneyland, the one I dreaded was the ratcheting of a roller coaster. The car was being pulled straight up; closer to the inevitable drop. Everything always ended in a fall.

"This ride is awesome," Peter yelled over the background noise.

"And not in a good way," I agreed.

"That's because you haven't done it with me," he said. I couldn't help thinking of the other things we hadn't done together.

Soon we were flying through the dark, highlighted by streaming strands of multicolor lights.

My stomach tried to reject my marshmallow treat. I swallowed it back down and closed my eyes against the lights. Worse. Sudden drops and turns flung me around against Peter who laughed and shouted "Woo-hoo!" But I couldn't think of him or anyone except how much I needed the ride to end.

During the longest thirty-five seconds of my life, I had time to question my marriage, my sanity and whether or not the sweet treat would end up on my lap. The only answer I received was when I stumbled off the ride and veered into the ladies room. I wouldn't have to worry about the calories of that particular snack.

Chapter 30

Ten minutes later I was stretched out on a concrete bench next to the Star Wars gift shop while Peter made his tenth call in five minutes spreading the word to his friends that he was New York bound.

Running away with Peter would solve everything. I could live rent free and travel to Walt Disney World and all points east. And I wouldn't have to face Michael at all.

All I had to do was give up my parent's home and spend the rest of my life hiding.

Peter pulled me up and I was afraid he was ready to spin me around again when Colin's voice boomed from behind me.

"I'm sure that Mini doesn't need you tossing her around anymore," Colin said. "She looks a little green."

"He's excited. He has great news." I tried to act cool while I detached Peter's hands that were linked under my breasts, pushing them up to my chin. I prayed Peter wouldn't share the news about taking me with him.

"Yeah!" Peter cried. "I've got a part on Off Broadway!"

"Congratulations," Colin smiled for the first time since Peter showed up. "So you'll be leaving us?"

"At the end of my shift tonight," Peter said.

"Great!" Colin looked at his watch. "Then you'd better report to your supervisor and let her know what's going on."

"Sure!" Peter hugged me again, and then ran off with a shout, "See you at the parade Mini!"

Colin stared at me with the expression Dad used when he waited for me to explain something I had done. Some kind of mistake I had made.

I was saved from trying to think of what to say when Felicity arrived.

"How'd your day go Mini?" Felicity asked.

"Oh yeah! Just a second," I unfolded the map and crossed out the last circle. "There! I finished every ride, shop and attraction at Disneyland. It might not be the most important thing that could have been accomplished today, but for me it's good. The first thing I can remember finishing in a long time."

"That's wonderful," she said. "Now if Colin doesn't need you, we need to get to the Castle and start packing before it's time for you to change for the parade."

I turned to Colin who stared at me. I had no idea what he thought, but I wanted to wrap my arms around the man who'd helped me finish and squeeze. He stuck his hand out and stopped me.

"Thank you," I said instead and shook his hand. "I couldn't have done it without you."

"Yes, you could have," Colin said. "But I was happy to be here. If I don't see you again, it was nice meeting you. Goodbye."

Piles of things I'd have wanted to say to Colin flashed through my brain. Could we be friends? Maybe see each other again at the park? He was even more fun to spend a day with at the park than my parents. Colin didn't give me a chance to ask.

"He's a strange man Felicity," we watched Colin disappear into the crowds. "Just when I am getting to know him, he changes."

"I was thinking the same thing," Felicity said. "We have to get to the Castle."

I'd learned so much today. I tossed the paper towel into the trash and looked back at Space Mountain before I refolded the map into a precise square. I would frame it as a reminder of what I could accomplish if I tried—and a reminder that just because something was thrilling, it was not necessarily good for you.

Back in the Castle room for the last time, I stared at the piles of clothes and items I'd picked up in two days. I had turned out to be quite a shopper after all. I had several fights on my hands with Michael. At the least, I wanted to be armed with my new things to remind me of the joy in the world.

Felicity had also sent up a matching set of pink mouse print luggage. *That will come in handy no matter which future awaits me.* She helped me pack the four logo-stamped bags with my new wardrobe. I was leaving the Castle tonight.

"Are you all right dear?" Felicity asked.

"Fine," I sputtered and tossed the beige clothes that no longer emotionally fit into the trash, then held my hands up to give up. "Well, not yet. But I hope to be."

"That's a mature answer." Felicity pulled my clothes out of the wardrobe for folding. "You've had a full day."

I picked up my bag and stuffed in my new sunglasses and the prize paperwork. "I still have a long day left, I'm afraid. Any suggestions?"

"Your future is yours to decide," Felicity held my hand. "We all have to balance many things at once. What we want, what others in our lives want, and what simply has to be done. I'm sure you'll figure out the right way to go."

"Based on all the right decisions you've seen me make?" I shook my head.

"Based on the growth I've seen in three days. You arrived here a woman with no idea of her own worth. No idea of what her place in the world was meant to be."

"I still don't know what I'm supposed to do tonight." I slipped the paperwork out of the prize envelope. "But you might as well show me where to sign."

"There'll be plenty of time after the parade," she said. "Let's get going."

When the last bag was placed near the door for a bell man I started to fill out the luggage tags. I added my name, but couldn't fill in the address.

I could escape with Peter. There wasn't anything at home I needed. I was already packed up and ready to leave from here. I had started out a singer. Maybe I still could be. It would be the easy way out.

I gave in to one more look out over Main Street, but before I reached the window, a light caught on my wedding ring from the nightstand where I'd cleared out my wallet. I didn't want to be a person who lets go of their wedding vows as if they never meant a thing. Even if there was not much left of them.

"I'll wait for you outside," Felicity said with a hug.

The joy of the space filled my senses once more— the soft touch of the gossamer bed curtains, the lacy pillows and the sweet scent created by the Minnie

Mouse bath products. I said goodbye to the room one last time and slipped the ring back on.

Chapter 31

The large gold hands of the Small World clock ticked along with the beat of my heart as I ducked into the backstage dressing room. In less than sixty minutes I would be driving Michael's car back to see what remained of my home after Hurricane Jessica and a flood of lies.

Each layer of the Queen's costume, starting with the silky white pantaloons, helped pull me into the present and away from fear of the future.

Stepping into the full hoop skirt and being laced up tight transformed my posture to a royal stance in front of the full length mirror. *You have to be different in this dress.*

My hair was tucked under a wig of the same color, but taller and heavier when pinned. By the time the crown was added to the top, I was six feet tall on the outside and ten feet tall on the inside.

I closed my eyes and wished that time would stop. Freeze in this moment. When I opened my eyes again people were still moving about, unaware that these were my last minutes as queen.

The dress didn't just fit my body. The intricate velvet dress was a second skin—a perfect fit. Every step mattered. The dressers showed me how to walk without tripping on the layers of petticoats that had been added since the last time I tried it on. I lifted the

207

skirt to glide to my float, but the hoop had a mind of its own and rocked back and forth like an overactive bell.

I lined up behind Pinocchio and the Blue Fairy, waiting my turn to board my float.

"I'm so nervous," I said to Pinocchio's plastic head while the familiar butterfly sensation of stage fright grew in my stomach.

Pinocchio nodded.

"Today's a big day for me," I rattled off to the poor actor playing the part of the puppet who wanted to be a real boy. "My first float and all."

Pinocchio patted my arm with his thick-gloved hand, maintaining his silent character mode.

"I wish I knew what to do with my life," I babbled, unable to stop talking. "I mean I could run away with the Prince or go home like a good girl."

Pinocchio struck a Thinker pose—a tiny plastic Thinker pose. He was either trying to figure out my dilemma or how to get away from the crazy woman.

"This is unreal." I waved to the backstage area full of garden planting pots and bits and pieces of replacement Disney. "How I wish this was my real life."

Pinocchio rocked back on his feet and pointed to the fairy who was listening.

"To be real," she waved her wand in front of me and said in a high soprano voice, "you have to be honest and true. Do the right thing."

"Whatever that is," I said while a crew member helped me up the temporary stairs to the floor of the float. The piped music grew louder as I was buckled around the waist against a backrest that was covered

208

with fabric. At my feet, two women attached the hem of my skirt by Velcro to yards of matching fabric puddling around me.

"Are you ready?" one yelled over the music.

"For what?" I asked.

She waved a small box that looked like a remote control. I couldn't hear what she said but she pointed to me and then the sky.

The float jerked forward to start and the woman made a sign to let me know she was about to touch the button. I got it. What I didn't get was what that was for. In the time it took for her to release her finger from the control I was lifted into the air about fifteen feet.

Fear was replaced by awe as I was raised high enough to see above the floats in front of me and all the way to Main Street. And on my right, the clock. Fifty minutes until my dream was over. I didn't want to waste them. For the first time in my life I grabbed the oxygen mask first. I wasn't going to give my last park minutes to Michael. I would save them for myself.

The float cleared the park entrance. Colin stood at the gate and looked up at me and smiled. Today he'd been my friend. And I had one chance to be queen.

The float teetered and I grabbed a safety bar as we turned the corner.

Minutes into the ride and my cheeks ached from smiling at the crowds all applauding the queen. The biggest winner ever.

Peter danced in front of the float with Snow White. He twirled her back and forth in and out of my view across the street lined with families and children. Performing was natural for him. Going with him, my life would be light and easy.

I tried to make eye contact with everyone. Taking in the families and the fantasy of the park I'd made mine today, my smile grew with each block of the parade. I understood my parents' gift. They had left me a home. Not just the wood and stone building in Anaheim Hills. I waved with both arms.

I wanted to share this moment with everyone. But mostly with my family. It was because of them that I was here. I didn't need them in my head anymore. They were in my heart forever.

"Mom and Dad," I said aloud, knowing my voice would not carry over the crowd and the music. "Thank you so much for giving me Disneyland. A place that feels like my own. A place to turn to. A home."

Chapter 32

Flipping up my hoop skirt I flashed layers of crinoline and pantaloons at the kids in Goofy's Jumping House when I squeezed through the small gate at Mickey's house for my last picture before abdicating my throne.

Mickey, dressed in a tuxedo, waited on the front steps of his house.

"Hi Mickey." He bowed and bent his large plastic head over my hand. I kissed his smooth cheek and he folded his hands over his face in mock embarrassment. *I am completely and utterly happy as I continued to float on the afterglow of the parade.*

"The photographers have asked to start in Mickey's garden," Felicity said.

We moved into the bed of giant plastic vegetables. Goofy joined us between the carrots and cauliflowers while the sound of the cameras snapped like swarming bees.

Goofy enveloped me into a huge hug and I smiled through tears at all the wonderful things that were happening. Before he touched my waist with his huge gloved hands I sensed it was Peter.

I smiled out to the growing crowd of faces. Small children, straining at their parents' hands to reach Mickey. Such happy faces. Anxious, excited, full of joy. All but one. Michael.

211

Anger, fear and inadequacy created an instant knot in my throat as a new emotion fought to take over.

My husband stepped close enough to cover me in a sticky layer of guilt. I moved away from Peter.

"I'm sorry," I managed to squeak out of my tight throat. I avoided looking at his eyes—the pair that had deemed me unworthy of faithfulness. "I should have told you the truth right away."

"That's all right, darling," he took me in his arms for a warm hug, starting a shock wave combining my desire to have been enough for him with a growing nausea tied to a vision of my going back to him. I pulled myself free hoping distance would clear my head. Goofy tapped one large blue foot. "It's understandable," Michael added. "It's not every day you win such a huge prize."

"What?" I waited for one of his rants. "I thought you'd be angry."

"Well of course I was worried," he said, then whispered in my ear. "But I can imagine how excited you were."

"Uh, thanks." *This was so not one of the possible scenarios I'd gone through in my head.* Michael waved to the crowd and I glimpsed the fun-loving man I'd met in college.

"Now we can start a family," he announced, spreading his hands out like he was on stage.

After all these years? Were all of my dreams coming true? I pictured sharing Disneyland with my child, pushing my own stroller down Main Street. And then my vision dropped to Michael's shoes. Three days ago he'd worn the same loafers out of the park with another woman.

He snaked one arm over my shoulder and spoke out as if he'd been invited to give a speech. "My wife is the grand prize winner. And with that money we can finally have a few kids."

I wanted a family. But if I were going to start a new life, I couldn't do it by letting Michael call all of the shots. I pushed one of his arms down and whispered. "We have so much to talk about first."

"We sure do," he broadcasted. Goofy, and Felicity had moved a discreet distance back and the photographer was still snapping photos of Mickey. "I read all about the entire prize on the internet. Of course we'll have to plan well—keep it status quo for a while. We don't want to fly into anything without charting a perfect course. But in five or six years we should be ready to take off with that family."

A picture of my future self waiting for Michael to decide my path flashed in my head. A light bulb didn't glare in my brain illuminating my future. But there was a sense of the slow rise of the sun. It dawned on me that it wasn't a new life he offered.

I didn't want to go back to the old life. Not just because he'd cheated, but because I didn't like that version of me. I didn't want to continue to be the one who waited for life anymore. I wanted a new adventure with friends, family and Disneyland.

"Look Michael," I pulled him to the side of the faux garden with the least amount of people while I summoned up the courage to rationally explain what I thought. "I agree we have a lot of things to work out before kids, but the same old way isn't going to work for me anymore. I've changed in the last three days. I want more in my life. Starting with the full Grand Prize."

Michael cocked his head to one side and bit his lower lip. His anger started to boil, but I stood firm, trying on confidence for size, hoping he couldn't tell how bad I shook under my royal velvet.

"The real prize is the travel," I added, my voice speeding up. "It's worth much more than the cash value. We should use that time together to see if we can get back to where we started."

"I am not," he paused for apparent emphasis, "going to traipse around the world playing child's games. I have a real job. Take the buyout."

I looked into his brown eyes and didn't melt. I saw a man who would never give me what I needed. If my life was going to work with anyone, I had to be happy with myself.

"But I already signed," I told what I hoped would be my last lie. "I took the prize. Not the cash. We can travel the world together with all those vacation days you never use. Get to know each other again. Then when I get a job we can be a real team."

Michael surprised me. He didn't explode. Not all at once.

"Get a job? You've never finished anything in your life," he sneered.

My feet froze and my posture unfolded from coward to queen. "That's not entirely true. I have finished something. I went on every ride and to every event and display at this entire park. I've been scared and sick and happy. It's been the best time in my life since mom and dad died."

"You mean since the day you married me?"

214

"No," I stood my ground, hoping that the tiara gave me an air of respect. "I am referencing the day my parents' died. I've been thinking about them non-stop for three days. Their death and their life."

"We're heading home to talk to our lawyer." His voiced dropped into a growl. "Anything you signed can be undone. Take off that ridiculous dress. We're leaving."

He took my arm and pulled, but this time my feet had another plan.

"I can't leave," I quivered, wishing my voice sounded stronger. "I'm meeting Mickey for one last photo shoot, the way I did with Mom and Dad."

Michael's coloring deepened to an angry red, matching the hue of the enormous radishes at his feet.

"You've completely lost your mind," he hissed. "I don't know what you've been doing here for three days, but this ends now. We're out of here Margaret."

I dropped my head and gravity threatened to spill the tears that had built up. I needed to leave before he caused a bigger scene.

The photographer walked past us. "Another picture by the gate," he pointed with his camera. He might have been the only one in the park who hadn't heard Michael's tantrum.

The tick twitching over my husband's left eye pulsed out his anger in Morse Code. A slight snap of his head told me he expected me at his side. Then a gloved hand took mine. Mickey.

"Get out of here. I'm talking to my wife," Michael yanked my arm with one hand and with the other pushed Mickey to the side, forcing my oldest friend to trip over a plastic carrot growing out of the ground, and land on his tail.

Then a blur of lime green and red flashed past me. Goofy tackled Michael to the ground, rolling between rows of gigantic cabbage sprouts.

"Peter," I cried, pulling on his long flapping ears as he punched Michael with ineffective thick gloved hands. Michael raised a fist and swung at Peter, knocking himself free.

Michael picked up a giant carrot that had broken off and raised it over Mickey's head while he was still struggling to get back on his feet.

"No!" I threw myself between them, expecting to take the blow for my dear friend when the wires of my hoop skirt managed to trip up Michael's feet and we both landed hard. I was on top, but upside down as my skirt inverted and my slippered feet kicked the air.

Strong hands grabbed my ankles and I was uprighted into the face of Colin.

He scanned my body like an x-ray machine, then moved me aside and he had one foot on Michael's chest. But it was a sniffling sound that drew me around.

The ten-second fight was witnessed by a large crowd. The happy, small smiles had widened into large, frightened O's.

"Okay friends," I croaked and thought of how to save the pristine memory of the park for the children. "Let's see who won this battle. Our vegetable thief?" I pointed at Michael who looked back at me as if I'd grown horns.

"Boo!" the kids cried.

"Our hero Goofy?" My voice quivered as I put a stake in the ground I'd never be able to pull out.

216

"Yay!" they cried.

"Our Disneyland officer will see that our thief is taken care of," I helped Mickey to his feet and then followed Colin, Goofy and Michael to a staging area behind the house.

Colin had appeared to have a few stern words with Peter, though I couldn't hear. It was hard to tell his reaction since Peter still wore the Goofy head.

"We're going to press charges against these characters," Michael spit out and his hands were cuffed by one of two security guards who had appeared. "Then they'll change the terms on that prize and we'll get the cash."

"But Michael," I cried, "you can't sue Disneyland."

"Watch me," he said.

"Not so fast," Colin said. "You have attacked two of our employees. You'll have to go with these gentlemen so they can complete a police report."

"This is ridiculous," Michael shouted. "I stood there minding my own business when they went crazy and attacked me. Right Margaret?"

Michael stared at me and I forced myself to meet his eyes. I was no longer ashamed or afraid. Nobody messed with my friends.

"He started it all," I pointed at Michael. "He also twisted my arm." I pulled up the velvet sleeve high enough for the red welts to show.

"You can't do this Margaret. I'll sue you. I'll take you for everything you have!"

He could. He could take Mom and Dad's house and tie up my prize forever. He could ruin the rest of my life, if I let him.

"Give me a minute with him first, please," I said and walked up close enough to Michael so no one but him could hear me.

A new confidence that had been building in me all day, coupled with knowing his hands were tied behind his back allowed me to speak clearly and without fear.

"I saw you kiss Jessica before you both left the park."

Michael's eyebrows shot up, then he squinted at me and smiled. "Babe, you're upset about something you think you saw?"

"I didn't think I saw anything. I know I did. You kissed her. Long and hard. I know what a kiss looks like," *and feels like*. "Why did you come back? For the money?"

"You're my wife," he said. "We're going to go back home and forget any of this happened."

I'd revealed the big secret and it hadn't had any effect on him at all.

"I can't do that Michael," I exhaled, feeling the courage to be honest. "I've changed. I don't like who I've been. I'm starting to find a new me. And it's exciting. You can try to be part of it or we're over. I can't go backwards."

"You can't leave me," he hissed. "You have no way to support yourself. And I'll get half of everything! The house and this stupid prize."

"You can't take everything," I shook my head. "Not after you gave nothing. It wouldn't be fair. Especially after you cheated."

"You've always been prone to daydreaming," he shook his head like I was a child caught making up a story.

218

"Our life together is over," I said. With each word, the heavy pounding in my heart lightened. "Here's what is actually going to happen. After you are released, you are going to go back to the house, pack up your things and go."

"Like hell I will."

"And you will not take my parents' house," I concentrated on what I wanted and tried not to focus on Michael.

Confusion crept into Michael's expression, but before he talked his way around my plan, I played my last card. If Michael knew that what I was about to say was based on a lie, he would have been so proud of me. I took a deep breath and hoped to steal his Salesman of the Year trophy for my performance.

"In return for your cooperation," I said, "I will not tell your boss that you are sleeping with his baby girl so you can keep the only job you've ever had."

"You wouldn't dare Margaret," he said, but I saw the same fear creep into his eyes as when his father was around. "What would my parents say?"

"That their son is a cheater?"

"You can't prove that."

I exhaled and let go of all the pain that had built up during my marriage. He was ugly. In his heart and mind. There was no part of him that I wanted any more. Under any circumstances.

"You mean with all the video surveillance at this park, you don't think my new friends couldn't come up with a little footage from the park exit?" I didn't smile or sneer, just stated the facts.

Michael opened his mouth, then closed it after no sound came out.

219

I took my first step away from him and added, "And Michael, the name is Mini. Check?"

He didn't struggle as the two security guards walked him through the doorway and toward Disney Jail. *The only place I haven't been to.* My new gal pals would be so jealous.

Chapter 33

Large gloved hands touched my shoulders and I turned into Goofy and cried what remained of my makeup into his red Hawaiian shirt.

A crackling sound at my ears told me his pillowed hands petting my head had enough polyester in them to make the hair of my wig stand on end in the dry summer heat. But the contact was comforting.

"Dobie's Bad Mini," he murmured.

"What?" I stood back and looked into his round blank eyes.

Peter pulled off the Goofy head. His blond hair plastered with sweat to his head, and yet he was still the most handsome man I'd ever seen up close.

"I said don't be sad, Mini," Peter repeated and smiled. "This couldn't be better."

"Are you kidding me? I caused a scene in front of dozens of impressionable children that may scar them for life, got you in trouble with your boss and sent my husband to Disney Jail."

"You didn't do that. He did. You don't have to stress about leaving. We can go when you're ready. I'll be making enough to take care of you—at least for the next few months. After that something will come up. It always does."

"But what would I do?" I put on hold the reality that I was five years older and too plain to be his girlfriend.

"Do whatever you want. We can make it work. You could restart your singing career. You were born to be on stage." He pulled me into a full mouth-watering, stomach-flipping kiss that lasted long enough for me to think I could run away.

"I thought that once," I stood on knees of butter, "but I realize that is just part of me. I don't want to live worrying about the next gig or thinking of my career or myself all the time."

"Take all the time you need. Hang out if you want. Start my fan club," he laughed. "I'll take care of you."

He covered my neck in a series of fluttery kisses that should have sent my toes curling, but all I thought was 'Peter Peter pumpkin eater, had a wife and couldn't keep her, put her in a pumpkin shell and there he kept her very well.'

"I don't want to live in a shell anymore."

"What?" *Damn it! He's even sexy with his eyebrows pulled together in confusion.*

"I mean," the thoughts formulated in my head and I bounced between extremes, "I know that my old life isn't going to work anymore, but I don't know yet what it is I'm supposed to do."

I touched his warm, wet lips with my fingertips and continued. "You don't need a charm. You have talent. You are your own lucky talisman. I don't know what direction my life is going to go yet, but it would be wrong for me to run away toward someone else's dream without figuring out what is right for me."

"What do you want Mini?"

"I'll know it when it's right."

Peter's pout was the best compliment I'd ever received.

I squeezed his hand one more time, then watched him walk through the gate to the employee dressing area, mentally patting that great ass goodbye. Felicity appeared at my side.

"Are you all right?" Her face flushed. "I was so worried when I heard there'd been a fight."

"Everything's fine," I said.

"You don't look fine," Felicity reached up and adjusted my crown, which was about to slide off sideways. "What happened to that energetic and excited woman I saw this morning?"

"She's exhausted."

"So you let him go," she said.

"His kiss did wake me up to the fact that I am desirable," I said. "But he wasn't my prince."

Chapter 34

The train whistled and rolled into the station at the Main Depot. I walked past in my civilian clothes and fought the urge to climb aboard and circle the park forever. But I'd been watching life from the outside for long enough. All the good stuff happened on the inside.

I was thirty years old and I finally knew what I wanted.

Colin and Felicity waited near the exit in almost the exact spot I'd stood when I'd seen Michael kissing Jessica three days and one lifetime ago.

"What now Mini?" Colin asked.

"I don't know," I blurted, then slapped my hand to my mouth. "I'm not going to say that again."

"What do you want to do Mini?" Felicity asked.

I inhaled deeply and handed her the packet I'd signed before I'd taken my costume off. "I definitely want to keep my entire prize," I said. "But I'd like more."

Colin and Felicity each watched, waiting for me to continue.

"I don't want to be alone anymore," I said. "I love working with people. Will you hire me to work here? I can be a gardener or ride attendant or maybe sell popcorn?"

Colin shook his head. "I'm sorry, but I don't see that working out."

"I promise not to eat all the popcorn!" I said.

"That's not the only thing that would bother me," he said. "I know a bad fit when I see it."

I shrugged and pulled my bag up higher onto my shoulder and tried to place a smile on my face. "I understand," I looked at Felicity for a little support and she was also shaking her head.

"I agree," Felicity said. "Mini in food service would be a huge mistake."

Okay, so maybe I'd grow too large for people to see the cart.

"It was a lot to ask I know." I didn't like their answer, but at least I'd asked. "Who'd want a singer who'd been partially trained in nursing, teaching, languages and lawn care, but has nothing to show for it?"

"Actually Disneyland would," Felicity said. "You're the perfect ambassador."

"The perfect what?" I glanced between Felicity and Colin who were grinning while Colin pulled a pin off his lapel and handed it to Felicity.

"You won the bet Felicity," Colin said. "She would be a perfect replacement for you."

"We both won," Felicity pinned the Tigger with the black nose to her collar. "This finally completes my collection."

I tried to process what they were saying. Did they want me?

Bits of lights twinkled at the corners of my eyes, but instead of darkness I focused back on Colin's smiling face. "But I haven't held a job since college," I said. "Are you saying I could do this? Two days ago you thought I'd bring down the park."

"Of course you'd go through Disney College," Felicity laughed. "But there are things you can't teach. You can diffuse stressful situations and naturally put others first."

I looked at Colin for a negative comment, but he nodded his head. "You're a multilingual, popsicle-wielding nurse, and a singing ride therapist. You're actually over qualified."

"I can't believe it!" I felt as high as if I'd gotten off Indiana Jones and was running down the path through the cave to get back in line for another round. *There is another life out there for me. Do you see this Mom and Dad?*

The bell man pulled a cart with my suitcases up to me. "Where do these go?" he asked.

Oh yeah, I need to go somewhere. Michael was at the house packing and I didn't want to be anywhere near him.

"I have a day to kill," I said, then asked Felicity, "think you can get me into the Grand Californian? I want to see the other park."

"I'll see what I can do," Felicity said and walked off talking into her radio.

Colin followed me to the gate.

"Will you be returning?" the clerk's hand stamp hovered above my hand.

"Yes." The quick-dry ink cooled my skin. The name Goofy glowed under the small black light and gave me the courage to walk forward into Disney Walk.

The hand on my shoulder was Colin's.

"So," I asked without turning. "What does the E. stand for?"

He sighed deeply and whispered, "Elvis. My parents were big fans."

My shoulders shook and laughter burst out.

"That is exactly why I never tell anyone!"

I buried my face in my hands and released the last of my tears; both his hands were on my shoulders, kneading, soothing.

"Don't worry Mini. It's going to be okay. You're part of the family now." Colin turned me around and brushed the tears away with a light touch that sent quivers to my core. My stomach growled in unison with my libido. "Let's go get you some popcorn."

"You know me," I said to another for the first time in a decade. "But Michael was right about one thing. I do live in a fantasyland. In three days, I've thwarted a villain, been kissed by a prince, and am about to become a fairy godmother. My reality is Disneyland."

"In that case let me spend the rest of the day with you," he took my hand, "and I'll show you the difference between a prince and a king."

THE END

Thank you to the writers who have helped me along the way: Bonnie Lee, Patricia L. Henley, Carole Kelleher, Julie Carlson and Penny Warner.

***

And a special thank you to Walt Disney and the entire Disneyland crew during the nearly fifty years that I have been visiting the park.